STUFFED ANIMALS

Story #7

STUFFED ANIMALS

A Novella

SHANNON RAE NOBLE

Copyright © December 2018
Shannon Rae Noble
Second Edition Digital April, 2021
Second Edition Printing August, 2024
Story #7
Stuffed Animals
A Novella

All Rights Reserved. No part of this book may be used or reproduced in any manner whatsoever except in the case of brief quotations embodied in critical articles and reviews.

This book is a work of fiction. Names, characters, places, and incidents are products of the author's imagination or are used fictitiously. Any resemblance to actual persons, living or dead, events, or locales is entirely coincidental.

Published by Crow 99 Books
PO Box 295
Port Crane, NY 13833

Cover by Taylor Alyson Butchko
@tayloralysonart

ISBN: 978-1-7321793-5-6

For Arnold John Schink.
The Eagle has landed.

One

Twilight drops its shadowy veil as I pull into the gravel drive. The A-frame is brightly lit from within, welcoming me home. Grey smoke curls up from the chimney, salting the chill air with the scent of wood fire.

I park in front of the garage's right bay and exit the Jeep, slamming the door firmly behind me. I stand for a moment, inhaling deeply.

It is just over forty degrees as the sun begins to dip behind the hills. Forty is warm compared to the unforgiving single digits and negative numbers that have assailed us this winter in Upstate New York; but this is still the chill, damp temperature of spring, as opposed to autumn's dry and balmy forty. Cold radiates from lumpy white mounds that are piled up along the sides of the driveway from the winter plowings. The ground is wet and cold where they've melted down.

I shiver in my winter camouflage.

The outside light beside the A-frame's front door flares into life. The door opens, and against the backlight stands the tall, imposing silhouette of a man.

He descends the steps. My heart skips a beat.

"Who are you and what are you doing in my house?" I say, trying to sound strong and unafraid.

"I can't tell you that," he answers. "If I do, I will have to kill you."

In the growing darkness, I see that he carries a large axe in one hand. He lifts it and smacks the back of the axe head against the palm of his hand as he advances.

"If you leave now, I won't call the police," I try again. I am bluffing, though. I can't call the police. I do not own a cell phone; there is only the land line inside the A-frame, and I will have to get past him to get to it. My chances at succeeding are slim to none.

"Why would I leave?"

I back away as he comes closer. That axe looks really big.

The man bursts into a sudden flurry of motion, his body spinning around. He raises the axe and releases it with force as he comes to face me again. The weapon flies end over end toward me. I shriek, dodging out of the way, as the blade comes within a foot of my face. I can hear the hollow *whew-whew-whew* sound as it turns, cutting the air beside me. The blade makes a decided *thkk* sound as the metal buries itself in the target affixed to a tree about six yards behind me. The target is carved and painted in the ghoulish image of what a vampire is supposed to look like.

The man is a several inches taller than me, even though I am a good 5' 11". He bows low, and in a deep, booming voice, he intones, "You look upon Abraham Lincoln, vampire hunter. You are now sworn to secrecy of what you have just witnessed."

I clap my hands and crow with delight. "Oh, Mr. *President*, I'm so *sorry*, I didn't recognize you in the shadows!" My husband enfolds me in his arms, lifts me up, and spins around again, taking me with him this time. "You will pay for the oversight, Bishop MacArthur!"

I love Cameron's Benjamin Walker impressions. He practices and practices, working so hard to make them perfect. Just for me. He does it because he's jealous of my attraction to Benjamin Walker's acting in the movie. I am awed by his axe work and the way he rocks his fitted, pleated wool coat.

STUFFED ANIMALS

"But that isn't fair! You're supposed to be fair! *You're* the one who jumped out at *me*! Besides, you almost hit me this time, you showoff!" I laugh breathlessly as Cameron sets me down and kisses me. I entwine my fingers through the thick black curls at the nape of his neck. He smells faintly of Drakkar Noir and MacArthur Marinara.

A wave of images assaults my mind, accompanied by a blur of emotions that washes through me: A group of young children singing, a flare of pride and happiness, a quieting, then a deep sense of loneliness and longing.

I break from Cameron's kiss before his transmission overwhelms me. "I missed you, too!" I hug him close, leaning my cheek against the shoulder of his wool coat.

"I'm sorry," he whispers against my ear. "Just a slip."

"Uh huh," I say with just a hint of sarcasm. "But it's okay. You don't need to apologize. It didn't hurt."

Cameron is a transmitter. Some of our close friends feel that I possess the greater of our two gifts; but I am convinced that Cameron's ability to transmit images and emotions to others is a much greater gift than mine. Sometimes he gets overzealous and loses control of what he sends out. Having as intimate a relationship as we do creates the necessity for a delicate balance of awareness for both of us.

Cameron's gift has been passed down to him through the genetic code of his bloodline, as has mine. Being descended from the Pendragon is a bit more impressive than my relation to King Arthur's taxidermists; but my forefathers were just a touch more. My father, my father's father, his father before, and all the men of my family practiced the art of re-vivication. They were re-animators; resurrectors. There have even been hints that my ancestors were present at Christ's resurrection. I don't know how much I believe that, but my family's distant ancestry is murky and buried in myth and legend, and it goes so far back that the only people who really know – knew – were the originators of our line.

My father wanted a boy. He got me, instead, but he still named me Bishop – a name he had chosen for the son that hadn't materialized. I'm sure it didn't hurt when he discovered that I possessed the family gift: the first female of my bloodline to exhibit it – that he was aware of. Heartened at the revelation, he set to teaching me all that he knew.

Cameron rests his hands on my arms, steps back, and looks at me. "Billy Tanner," he states.

"I know."

Billy Tanner is, as his surname proclaims, a tanner. I've spent the better part of the day with him, as I had skins that needed preparation. I smell strongly of the Tannery – the convenient name of his workshop.

Cameron drapes an arm across my shoulders and guides me to the front door. "To the shower with you, then. Food is almost done. How is the fourth-time father?"

"He is ecstatic because he finally produced a boy."

"I can picture him jumping for joy."

We cross the threshold. I turn my back to Cameron and shrug out of my camouflage. He takes it from me and hangs it on the rack, then slips out of his own wool coat and hangs it beside mine.

He looks far too comfortable in a plain grey t-shirt and green and blue flannel lounge pants. A pristine white apron with frilly trim completes the ensemble. He pulls his dark-framed glasses from his apron pocket and holds them up to the light, inspecting the lenses for dirt and smudges, then puts them on.

He looks incredibly sexy. The color of his t-shirt brings out the unearthly color of his tawny eyes. They shimmer like golden metallic crayons. They are widely spaced above his long, crooked nose. His pale skin stands out starkly against his unruly jet black curls. His mouth is wide, and he smiles at me with a model's perfect white teeth.

Cameron isn't handsome. He is striking.

"What are you looking at?" he asks me.

My words echo my thoughts. "My incredibly sexy husband." I sit on the bench and unlace my boots.

I often turn the idea over in my mind that he is an alien guest from another planet. Sometimes he looks beyond human.

This is one of those times that I am grateful that Cameron is not a receiver. I don't want him to catch this thought and be hurt by it, even though it isn't a negative one. Not to me, anyway.

STUFFED ANIMALS

He removes my camouflage cap, releasing the two thick red braids stuffed loosely inside it. He tries to run his fingers through them to separate them into their unruly curls, but his fingers catch in the tangles.

He wrinkles his nose. "You are *aromatic*. My eyes are watering."

"Fine, fine, I'm going. But you know you wouldn't have me any other way," I tease. "Back in twenty."

A shower is just the thing I need after being at the Tannery all day. I am scrubbing vigorously when the shower door slides open and Cameron steps in. He moves close behind me and whispers in my ear, "I'll help you wash your back."

"What about the MacArthur Marinara?"

"It's done. It will wait."

I hand the sudsy loofah to him over my shoulder. I know that he wants to wash off all traces of Billy Tanner.

The rough sensation feels good on my back. A sweet floral scent rises in the steam around us. I close my eyes and let my mind empty, sinking into the moment beneath the spray of hot water. The feel of the loofah disappears, replaced by the sensation of Cameron's palms sliding down my back and around to my belly. He pulls me against him, and I lean against his chest. I tip my head back to meet his kiss.

His shield is up, blocking any unwanted transmissions. I am met with warm velvety darkness and the sense of safety, of security. I lose myself in the press of Cameron's body against mine and his hands upon my skin.

Two

*F*riday morning, after Cameron leaves for work, I take the Jeep over to Stuffed Animals to deliver three mounts, plus one that was supposed to have been mounted, but instead, sits on my shoulder during the ride, grinding strands of my hair in his beak. His name is Jon, and he is a raven. He is the companion of Samantha Smith, a long-time friend of my family. Sam is in her late 70s, and Jon has kept her company for nearly half of her lifespan.

When she brought him in for mounting, I performed Special Services instead, as a surprise to Samantha.

"Hey, Soph!" The bell jingles, and I hold the glass door open with my foot as I squeeze myself through with Demetrios, Ophelia Jennings's cat.

Sophia Darling emerges from the back room and rounds the counter. "I'll get that!" she takes the Siamese from me. "How is Jon doing?"

"He seems to be recovering just fine."

"He looks great!"

"Thanks! I have two more standards in the Jeep."

She props the door open and follows me. She helps me carry in a mink and a badger.

STUFFED ANIMALS

We arrange the new mounts among my personal display animals in front of the plate glass windows. We step outside to the Main Street sidewalk.

I stand back to view my work. My animals always look different in the storefront than they do in my workshop. Though I am not fond of fluorescent lighting, I use it in my workshop to make sure I can do my detailed work. Here, in the natural light, they take on new life.

"I did do a good job, didn't I?"

"Kickass job!" she smiles, and we high-five.

"Kickass, kickass!" Jon says. "Good job!"

I look around the store. As always, it looks immaculate; no dirt in the corners, and the front display windows are so clean that it is easy to forget they are even there.

Sophia is my right-hand girl. I know I can count on her to keep everything shipshape, from professionally maintaining my storefront to managing the taxidermy's finances. Her presence allows me to concentrate on my work. She takes care of everything else.

She returns behind the counter. She sweeps her thick, jet-black hair behind her neck as she peruses the message book. "So you have some calls to return. Orders are picking up." She grabs a separate piece of paper and looks up at me with bright blue eyes from beneath the thick fringe of her bangs. "This lady stopped in. She wanted to speak with you about Special Services." She slides the paper across the counter.

A name and phone number are penned on the paper in spidery handwriting. "Elspeth Sinclair?"

"She was a strange one. She didn't look right. Weird, old-looking clothes – like not even from this century. Her skin was white as a sheet, and her face was like – doughy. She wore a lot of makeup, and it didn't seem like she knew how to apply it correctly. Clownish, almost."

"Did she say who referred her?"

"No, she just walked in and asked about Special Services. She wrote that note and asked for 'the taxidermist' to call her."

"I don't like how this sounds. If she stops in or calls again, please tell her my schedule is booked. I have no openings for new clients." Looking at the message book, I reflect that this is not untrue.

"Okay, will do."

I step behind the counter into the back of the shop, which houses the office, a kitchen with a small table and chairs, and the bathroom. "How are the numbers looking?"

"Pretty good," she says. She hands me a thin stack of paperwork, which proves to be last month's reports. I glance through them, then hand them back.

"I'm out," I tell her. "I'll see you again in a few days.

"Okay. Have a good weekend."

"You enjoy your weekend, too!" I ask the raven on my shoulder, "Do you want to see your Mom?"

"Mam. Sam! Wham bam, thank you, Sam!" Jon says. *"Kickass!"* I grin at Sophia and give her a small wave.

We drive to Sam's single-wide, which is situated on five acres just outside of town. When I open the Jeep's door, Jon flies out, up to the porch. He taps on the outside storm door as I climb the steps.

"Mam! Sam! Wham, bam, thank you, Sam!"

The inner door flies open. "Jon? Jon!" I jump back as the storm door swings wide and Sam bursts out, displacing Jon, who flutters his wings and lands on her shoulder.

"Bishop! Is it really Jon? I can't believe you did this!" Sam's joyful expression is cross-crossed with a web of age lines etched into her skin. Her steel-grey hair glints brightly in the sunshine.

"Kickass!" Jon agrees.

"Is it okay, Sam? That I did it? I wanted to surprise you, and I was hoping that it would be okay."

"Are you kidding?" The tiny woman grabs me and squeezes me tight, her strength belying her size and her years. "I love you for it! Is he healthy? Is he normal?

"He seems right as rain. He recognized me, he recognizes you. He eats, preens, flies. I think he will be just fine. But if any issues crop up, please call me right away."

"Okay, Bishop. Thank you! Thank you! There are no words to tell you how grateful I am."

"I can see it, Sam. You don't need to try to tell me. Enjoy."

STUFFED ANIMALS

* * *

I wake on Saturday morning to the sound of a steady but gentle rain tapping on the A-frame's slanted roof. I open my eyes and see the grey morning light that descends into our loft bedroom through the rain-blurred skylight. According to the position of the black filigree hands against the white clock face seated on my bedside table, it is a few minutes after seven.

I rub my eyes, yawn and stretch beneath the blankets. Feeling Cameron lying beside me, I move so that the entire length of my body is pressed against his warm skin, from shoulder to ankle. He stirs, opens his eyes, turns to face me. He slips one arm beneath my neck so that my head rests on his shoulder. I drape my leg over his hip. He pulls me close and kisses me.

I feel him stir beneath the blankets, his hardness pressing against me. I let myself sink against him, wrap my arms around him and move in closer as he nudges between my legs, aligning for entrance. I open wider for him and he pushes in gently, finding his fit, then more firmly, with a long, slow, steady slide that almost fills me. He strokes once more, hard; my breath hitches in my throat as sensations start streaming through me when his touch meets me, deep inside.

He rolls me onto my back. His whisper is hot against my neck. "Are you ready?"

I know when he asks me this that he is going to open his floodgates: full transmission, no blocks in place.

This won't be everyday morning sex. It won't even be what is termed "good".

My husband is going to pull us outside of this plane.

This isn't something we've perfected. It is something we practice, that we experiment with. It is an experience that can't be done hastily, when time is short. It also requires my full trust in Cameron to keep me safe. To keep *us* safe.

But it's Saturday morning, still early, the weather is highly conducive to staying in bed, and we have nowhere to be. We can take our time.

And my faith in him is implicit.

Or at least, I'm pretty sure it is.

"Go," I tell him, and ready myself.

Tightly joined, we move together as the rain taps steadily on the roof.

I close my eyes, losing myself in the light that begins to wash through me in waves. Soon, the brightness is all-encompassing, close to blinding, and the waves build to one long, continuous wave, buoyed up by a constant pulse beneath that I can almost hear.

The feel of the bed propping up my body disappears, and I am floating, weightless. The only thing I can feel is the pleasure rippling through me and the solidity of Cameron's body wrapped within my arms.

My vision is gone. I can't see, I can only feel. I also hear: a soft, distant "boom", and another sound, a "puff", and a now a strange fizzing sensation, as though I've become carbonated. The feel of Cameron's body is gone, and I am in the rain.

No – I *am* rain. I am falling in thousands upon thousands of vapor drops. My body is separating at the cellular level. All I have left is my consciousness. I don't know how I can even tell that I am mist, lacking the physical sensation.

The first small sense of fear seeps through me. I don't know where I am, where Cameron is, and I'm not even a human being anymore. We've never done this specific venture before, and I don't know if Cam can bring us back whole.

What if I am lost here forever? Falling through eternity as drops of water spray. Only consciousness, only thought, no body, for the rest of my days, which might stretch on and on and on in this state until my consciousness becomes insane.

I try to shut these thoughts out before full panic can take me, and I try to re-focus on what it feels like to float in this form.

Then comes the unfamiliar sense of a different kind of entry. Something sinks into the spaces between my misty drops, my cells, my atoms.

It is Cameron, in the same state as I. He fills all of the emptinesses in me in until there are none left.

He has somehow remade us into a single entity, shedding our separateness and individuality, our energies melding into one being. The profound sense of comfort, of belonging to one another, is thoroughly consuming, and my fears evaporate.

STUFFED ANIMALS

The pulse holding up the continuous wave slows and separates, and Cameron's particles lift away. I feel the echoing emptiness their absence leaves behind. I want them back, but I am high on the pleasure that takes me, washing through me, beat after slow, long beat. The moments stretch out into what seems like infinity.

Then we are back in our bed, tangled in the sheets beneath the loft skylight.

We are both covered in hot, slippery sweat. The heat between us is almost unbearable, but I don't let go. I keep my arms and legs clamped around Cameron as though my life depends on it, receiving his strokes as he thrusts into me with all of his strength.

The final wave melts upward through me, holding me inert and helpless against its impact. Filling me entirely, Cameron stays. I open my eyes, and he immediately captures my gaze with his own. He uses the connection to pull me higher internally.

"Stay there!" I whisper, gripping him hard to keep him from pulling away.

He holds his position, braced on his forearms. Beads of sweat drip off of his face onto mine, rolling down my cheeks into my already sweat-dampened hair.

His kiss is full, deep, and hot. We hold together.

He groans. I feel him let go, and it is he that now pulses inside of me. The sensation brings me higher and I climax again, pushing against him, low moans escaping the back of my throat. He collapses on top of me, breathing heavily into my hair, his body shuddering.

I close my eyes, let my body go limp, let the after tremors take me.

We lay together, cooling.

A woman suddenly appears in my mind's eye: She is elderly. A tailored wool winter coat wraps her short, dumpling form. A brocade scarf draped around her neck encircles her white blouse's high, frilled collar, which practically cups her loose double-chin. Her hair is a deep, nearly purple auburn, much darker than my flame-red curls, and it is piled loosely in an elaborate coiffure upon her head; wispy tendrils frame her face.

Her alert, dark brown eyes, nearly black, are scanning the scene that lies before her. She wears red lipstick on her aged, bow-shaped lips, and bright, circular spots of rouge adorn her white, powder-caked, doughy cheeks. A thick blue stripe covers each eyelid above extremely false eyelashes.

I drop a black veil over the image of her face, blocking her searching eyes, obscuring her from my vision and me from hers.

Cameron raises his head and looks at me. "Am I still good?"

"You are better than good," I manage to breathe. "That was literally out of this world!"

He lets his head drop onto the pillow. "It was a ride, wasn't it?"

I giggle breathlessly at his wording, but I feel just a tinge of fear. "It was. Do you – do you think that when we do that, we separate completely afterward? Or does part of us remain joined? Do we lose part of ourselves?"

"I have no idea. But I bet we'll find out."

"So you haven't done that before?"

"It was a surprise to me, too. That's the first time for both of us. I'm not even sure how I did it, or that I could do it again. For all I know, it may have been both of us together that did it, or maybe just you."

"I'm sure it wasn't me alone. I could almost believe it was both of us. My money is on you, though."

Cameron props himself up on his elbow and rests his head on his hand. He pushes my hair gently back from my forehead. "What's going on, Vix?" A thin, concerned line forms vertically between his eyebrows.

"I don't know. I thought I just saw something weird. Did you come in contact with an old woman at the school in the past few days? No, let me correct that. Did you come into contact with an *antique* woman?"

"Maybe. Grandparents' Day was this week. Why do you ask?"

"I saw an old woman looking out of your mind. Just now."

His expression becomes suddenly alert. "What?"

"You weren't aware of her?"

"No. What did she look like?"

"Short and thick, dressed eccentrically. Old-fashioned to the point of being Victorian. Lots of hair in a fancy do, piled very high on her head. Marge Simpson meets the psychic from 'Poltergeist'."

Cameron thinks for a moment, his tawny eyes losing focus as his thoughts turn inward.

"Heavy eye makeup, red lipstick." He lets out a deep breath and lowers himself to rest again. "Elspeth Sinclair fits that description. She's somewhat dowdy. She's the great-aunt of one of my students."

"I think she knows about you."

"You *saw* her?"

"Yes, I saw her face."

He looks dismayed, and he groans and smacks his forehead with his palm. "I didn't touch *her*. But her student ran up and grabbed my hand while Miss Sinclair was holding her other."

"Shit."

"Shit," he agrees. "I can't believe I wasn't aware of her! But maybe it was just a fluke. Maybe it was just a random memory that slipped through."

"It didn't feel that way. Her presence seemed deliberate. I think she was trying to pinpoint your location. And she has power."

We lapse into silence for a moment; then something dawns on me. "*Elspeth Sinclair*. Sophia gave me a note from a woman named Elspeth Sinclair. She came into the shop a few days ago. She wanted Special Services."

"It must be the same woman. 'Elspeth' isn't that common of a name, especially in this tiny burg."

"The woman I saw fits the description Sophia gave me."

He rests his head back down on my shoulder and drapes his arm across my body, hugging me close to him. "I'm sorry, Bishop. I spend so much time controlling what I transmit that I don't always remember to guard against people who may try to get in. They are so rare."

I could get angry. I could yell and scream and ask him how he could be so stupid as to let his guard down. But I can already feel his sadness and disappointment that he has let me down. Besides, I can't expect him to have two-way defenses in place, twenty-four, seven. Inside his classroom full of innocents, there isn't much for him to guard against. And on Grandparents' Day? There have never been issues

I decide to put the woman out of my mind for the time being. It is a beautiful rainy Saturday morning. I am curled up with my husband beneath the blankets, cozy and safe in our private sanctum. All is right with my world.

I'm not going to let Elspeth Sinclair spoil it. She didn't look intimidating, in the least.

I can't help but feel there is trouble coming, though.

Soon.

We lay together in a comfortable silence, listening to the morning rain. Eventually Jubilee Joe, our resident rooster, begins crowing outside.

I nudge Cameron. His weight is making my body go numb. "Okay, sleepy head. We need to get up. We have work to do."

"Yes, we do," he agrees. "I'm a little concerned about going up on the roof in the rain."

"Well, maybe by the time you get there, it will be dry. It's supposed to clear up."

He kisses me. "Good morning, Vixen. I love you."

I return his kiss. "Good morning, Mr. President. I love you back."

He looks into my eyes for a few seconds, then smiles. "Let's get out of this bed before we stay here all day."

We drag ourselves downstairs. I make the coffee and, ever the chef, Cameron makes us breakfast.

I love my husband.

Three

Outside, I stand at the edge of the front yard and pass my hand to bring up the light so that I can see the seals and sigils that cover the A-frame. They glow like blue fire against the dark wood and the gloom of the day. A few of the wards have faded, and the seals around the door and windows are frayed and bleeding at the edges.

Cameron and I have become complacent, forgetting that there are reasons why we take such measures against the outside world. It has been a few years since the last time a power hunter landed on our doorstep.

We don't use cell phones and we are not connected to the internet, except for the storefront, which isn't located on the property. Our only connections to the outside world are the cable for the big old television set and the rotary telephone that is still plugged into the wall. It rarely rings.

We are literally "off the grid". Our homestead is self-contained and self-sustaining, powered by wind, water, and solar alternatives that my father put in place. We have an extensive vegetable and herb garden, and we grow most of our fruits. We have a small orchard with apple trees, some pear and cherry trees; and our berry patches are plentiful. We keep our own small chicken coop. We still trade home-canned goods and fresh produce for beef and pork packages with the Sage Farm every few months, and we have also have a standing trade with Trunkle's Dairy.

Our homestead and our community's support of one another are multi-generational, started by my great-grandfather and grandfather when they founded Wilson Lake. The wards and boundary defenses on my family's twenty-seven acre property are also multi-generational, established when our two families settled the land.

Being a third-grade teacher, Cameron has significantly more exposure to society than I do. He relates more closely with his young charges than he does with their parents. He doesn't have any great love for parent-teacher conferences or the suffocating energy of a crowded auditorium during Christmas performances and the like. Thankfully for Cam, these events only take place a few times per year.

Cameron's loyalties lie with the children. He does what he loves, and a small touch of his gift enables him to instill a sense of compassion and empathy in his students; qualities that help to shape good human beings. Initially, I was apprehensive about the moral and ethical ramifications of him using his gift in the classroom; but after much reflection and discussion with my husband, I remembered that this is Cameron MacArthur. I have known him practically since birth. He is the most sensitive, gentle, intelligent man I have ever had the pleasure to know. He would never bring a child to harm.

Not intentionally.

Because Cameron is in town every day, he tends to do the grocery shopping and run the other household errands, which I am thankful for. Although I know and like most of Wilson Lake's residents, I can't handle a concentration of too many different personalities and energies at one time. It is overwhelming.

I enjoy the solitude of my workshop, which, like the rest of the buildings on the 27, was built by my great-grandfather. He built the big log cabin in the woods, with the smaller workshop close by. After Cameron and I married and my father and forefathers had all passed on, we disassembled the log cabin and moved the timber and other materials to a clearing closer to the edge of the woods and more accessible to the road. There, we built the A-frame. We left the workshop intact, and it became my own.

I visit the storefront once or twice a week. Sophia opens it for a few hours each weekday. She maintains my taxidermy's online presence. I have only a one-page site with basic information, an e-mail address, and a Facebook page; but Sophia manages it all. It is through these avenues that I receive the majority of my orders.

A very small percentage of my customers request Special Services. They are referred by word-of-mouth only. "Special Services" is a generic term for "reanimation". A select few members of the town know about my and Cameron's gifts, but we remain as discreet as we can. When someone unknown comes sniffing around town without a known and trusted referral, I don't do business with them, and I have Sophia turn them away.

This is why I refuse to deal with Elspeth Sinclair.

* * *

By the time Cam and I finish assessing what repairs need to be done, the rain has stopped and the sky has cleared. A bright yellow sun beams down from an infinite solid blue field. The droplets and rivulets left upon the slanted roof by the morning rain have evaporated in the quickly warming air. Cameron is up there now, re-setting our lightning rods and reinforcing the wards.

I use my salt, silver, and iron solution to repaint the sigils and wards and to seal the doors and windows. The solution becomes transparent when dry, rendering it virtually undetectable.

It is difficult work for me. My chemical makeup is extremely sensitive to iron. I am weakened by direct contact; it is almost like an allergy. I wear a mask and rubber gloves to apply the solution.

I have just finished reinforcing the French doors and the front windows when the phone rings inside. I lay down my brush and tray and wipe my hands on an old towel that I've brought out with my materials.

Inside, I lift the handset. "Hello?"

"Is this the taxidermy?" The unfamiliar voice sounds dry and papery.

I can feel the blood rush out of my face and each individual hair stand up on the back of my neck as a chill skitters down my spine.

Exactly eleven people have our landline number. The same eleven people have had our landline number since the phone was first put in, over sixty years ago.

This is not one of those people.

"I'm sorry?" I ask, taken aback.

"I am trying to reach the taxidermy shop," the voice says.

"I'm sorry. You have the wrong number."

"Oh," pause. "I apologize."

"Not a problem," I say as nonchalantly as I can.

Click.

I press the hang-up lever briefly and then dial Sophia at Stuffed Animals. "Hey Soph, did you give someone our phone number?"

"No. Why?"

"Someone just called here looking or a 'taxidermy shop'. Has anyone called there?" The line begins to crackle with static.

"No, not recently. I've given you all of the calls." More crackling, growing louder.

"Have you noticed anything out of the ordinary?"

"No. That weird old lady stopped in again, but I told her you were booked up. I didn't tell you because I figured it didn't matter; you weren't going to do business with her, anyway. Was that wrong?"

"Oh, no, no, Soph, you're fine. What did this old lady's voice sound like?"

"Um . . . old? Dry? And masculine."

"Okay. Thanks."

"I swear, Bishop, I didn't give her your number."

"I believe you, Sophia, it's okay. Keep an eye out for anything you feel is strange, would you? And take care."

"Yes, I will."

The static morphs into a sudden, loud screech. Startled, I nearly drop the handset into its cradle. Simultaneously, I hear a loud *crack* outside, followed by a series of thumps descending down the roof.

I run out the front door, down the steps, and around the corner, where I find Cameron lying still on the wet grass.

I drop to my knees beside him.

"Cam!" I slap his face once, lightly, then again, a harder. He does not respond.

There is a livid red mark on the right side of his neck. I pull back the collar of his blue button-down flannel, and I see that the mark travels down his neck to his shoulder. I fumble with his buttons, and then I just yank his shirt open, oblivious as to whether any of the buttons pop off. I push up his t-shirt to reveal his bare chest, and I gasp when I see the angry red lines that have spread across his skin over his right rib cage, up his chest and neck, disappearing beneath his shirt sleeve. The mark has a thick, raised central line, from which small scarlet branches spread out across his skin and end in feathery tips. The entire mark looks similar to the network of veins one finds on the underside of a leaf. Yellow burn blisters are bubbling up and expanding along some of the branches.

The right side of Cameron's body is also covered with swelling bruises. Blood trickles from a goose egg on his forehead.

"Cameron!" I shake him again, and his head just lolls. "Shit, shit, shit!" Tears sting my eyes and panic rises from my stomach into my throat in the form of burning bile.

I know that most of Cameron's injuries are the result of the impact of his fall, but I have never seen anything like the red markings before. The yellow blisters look like burns. I need to find out what happened to him so that I will know how to treat him.

I close my eyes and take a few deep breaths to calm and center myself against my apprehension. I can't protect myself much against anything Cameron has experienced, because I will feel it myself, from the inside out, not like something coming at me externally.

I am afraid it's going to hurt.

I place one hand on Cameron's bare chest. His transmissions are leaking freely in his unconscious state, and immediately upon our skin-to-skin contact, the images begin.

For a few seconds, I am Cameron, standing on the roof. The bright yellow sun beams down from the cloudless blue sky, feeling pleasantly warm on my skin, and a slight breeze eddies across my face and ruffles my hair. I am conscious of the various background noises: the insects buzzing in the yard, the birds chirping happily in the surrounding woods, and the chickens clucking contently.

I feel serene as I work, making sure the three lightning rods that are affixed to the A-frame's roof are straight and secured firmly. I use the portable etcher to re-etch into the metal the sigils that have been weathered smooth. I am just finishing up when I hear the phone ringing inside the house; hear the front door open and close as I, Bishop, go inside to answer it.

A moment later a loud hissing sounds above me. The noise is similar to the sound of high-pressure steam escaping from a pipe.

I look up into the sky and see a white trail crossing the infinite blue above me. I think that a plane must have recently flown overhead, leaving the white trail behind. But then, from the white trail, a bolt of lightning suddenly snaps down, striking the rod that I have just released a second ago.

I am too close to the rod to escape unscathed. The electricity crackles, dancing down the slim piece of metal and snaps out to engulf me where I balance on the roof.

The white-hot pain sears through me as the charge holds me captive for a few seconds. I try to break the connection with Cameron, try to yank my hand away, but I am held fast, frozen in the transmission. By the time the electricity has dissipated, I am unconscious, my limp body folding and rolling and bouncing down the length of the A-frame's steeply slanted roof.

As soon as I am able, I yank my hand away from Cameron's skin, still feeling the pain of the electrical jolt and multiple contusions from Cameron's fall.

So now I know that the red streaks and the yellow blistering are electrical burns.

STUFFED ANIMALS

Between these and the other injuries that he has sustained from falling off of the roof, Cameron requires immediate treatment. I must act first and work a fast healing ritual to repair some of the damage. There is no time to call the hospital and wait for an ambulance.

Still kneeling beside my husband, I concentrate on my knees and toes where they connect with the ground, separated by a layer of denim at the knee and by the leather upper and thick soles of my boots. The earth's cold wetness seeps up through its grass blanket into the denim of my jeans, making it hard for me to concentrate on pulling the healing energy up from the thawing earth.

My energy stores have depleted over the winter, and I haven't yet done any recharging. This early in the spring, when the weather is still often chill and inclement, I haven't had a lot of opportunity to plug into nature and replenish. It is easier in the warmer months, when I am able to dispose of the heavy layers of clothing and connect directly with the earth, water, and vegetation.

The energy lurches up through my knees in a thin stream, barely perceptible, then stops. I narrow my focus further, hoping to thicken the stream and increase the volume, but it doesn't seem to help. Cameron's marks and bruises barely lighten with the sparse amount of healing energy I am able to deliver.

Desperate, frustrated, and trying to keep panic at bay, I tug the laces of my boots loose and kick them off as my heart pounds double-time behind my ribcage. I pull off my socks and toss them aside. The frigid earth beneath the wet grass is cold enough to hurt.

I stand and wince, dig my toes and heels in, close my eyes and empty myself of all feeling, all emotion, all sensation. I empty my mind of all images, all thoughts, all fear. I breathe deeply, inhaling the scent of pine on the breeze. I feel the warm sun on my face, the top of my head, my shoulders. I listen to the whispering of the leaves on the trees.

Feeling more calm, my spirit quieting, I focus on the soles of my feet where they connect with the grass and beneath it, the newly thawed and rain-soaked earth. I breathe and concentrate on the connection. I send the entreaty from my heart and stomach down into the earth.

Healing a living being is much easier than reanimating one that has "died". The way reanimation works is to heal the body enough to keep the soul attached and intact, rather than trying to revive a cold, dead being whose soul has departed. There is only so much time that can elapse between death and the reanimation. Once the soul leaves the body, there can be no revivication. The main effort is to keep the soul from departing. Either way takes energy; but reanimation claims more, and the energy always comes from the same source: the living earth.

For those in doubt, it works better than CPR.

I know the energy has begun to flow when the soles of my feet begin to warm. I wait as long as I can, trying to keep the conduits as wide as possible, preventing any possible blockages to the stream. Eventually I fall back to my knees beside Cameron. I am unsure whether I have charged enough, but my instincts tell me that I can't afford to wait any longer.

I place my palms on Cameron's chest, covering the worst of the red markings and yellow blisters. I dig my bare toes into the earth beneath the wet grass. I quiet myself again and pull the energy up into my body and direct it out through the palms of my hands, into Cameron's skin.

I don't count. I just sit still, in the same position, breathing evenly and pushing the soft yellow light of healing energy into Cameron's chest. I don't know how long I sit there; but my eyes snap open when I hear Cameron groan.

"Cam?" My eyes scan his body for signs of healing. The bruises are still there, but they have taken on the greenish-yellow of partially healed contusions. The swollen spots have gone down, and the electrical burn blisters have nearly healed. The branched and feathered markings caused by the electrical discharge are no longer angry red, but have taken on the white coloring and puckered edges of healed scar tissue.

Maybe I won't need to call the ambulance.

"Bishop? What's going on?" Confusion clouds his light eyes.

"You don't remember?"

"I was on the roof. What am I doing here?"

STUFFED ANIMALS

"You fell, Cam. A lightning bolt struck the rod, and it jolted you because you were standing so close to it. You passed out and fell off the roof. Do you feel any pain? Can you move your fingers and toes?"

"Yeah. Give me a minute. I think I'm okay."

I offer him my arm as leverage to help him sit up. He has automatically collected his errant thoughts and put his block into place. The wall is weak, but it is there.

For the first time, I notice that something is missing. "Cam? Where is that harness you are supposed to wear when you're working on the roof?"

He rolls his eyes at me.

"Cameron MacArthur! Don't roll your eyes at me! Are you *trying* to get killed?" He looks away from me and a bright redness creeps up his cheeks. "I know it doesn't look cool, and you think you're invincible and all, but that harness is supposed to keep you *safe!*" I bite my lip, trying to hold back my temper. "I am tempted to leave you right here and let you take care of your own damn self!"

"I'm sorry, Bishop!"

"If you would start thinking, maybe you would stop doing things that you need to apologize for! What did you *think* would happen if you slipped and fell?"

He looks at me and gives me a sudden grin. "The slant of the roof is steep, and the edge isn't far from the ground. I figured I would just roll all the way down."

Speechless, I stare at him.

In that moment, I take a breath and I taste the fresh spring air, permeated with the scent of the surrounding pines, among which the chickadees flit and blue jays call. I become conscious of the warm sunbeams kissing my face beneath the pristine robin's-egg blue sky and the sound of the breeze blowing through the tree tops.

My anger dissolves, and I snort laughter. I nod at the roof. "*That* did not sound like a very smooth roll to me. It sounded more like a bounce. Actually, it sounded like *several* bounces."

Cameron begins to scramble to his feet. "Okay, help me up."

"Hey! Don't you try to use your influence to keep me from berating you, because you could have been *killed!* It isn't fair for you to try to mute my anger like that. My feelings are legitimate. What am I supposed to do if something happens to you?"

He puts his arms around me and pulls me close. "Nothing is going to happen to me. And I'm sorry."

"But something *did* happen to you! You fell off the damned *roof!*" I pull away from him and look at him, balled fists on my hips. He looks at his feet.

I sigh, exasperated. "Come on. Let's get you inside."

After a few moments, Cameron is settled on the sofa, ice packs adorning the few nasty bruises that are still apparent. The goose egg on his forehead has receded a bit.

I sit beside him. Afraid to kiss his face, I kiss the back of his warm hand and press it to my cheek.

"What is *that?*" he says. He pulls me to him and kisses me full on, and I know he is trying to make up for upsetting me.

Despite the improvements to his injuries, he still looks unwell. His face, which is normally pale, has lightened to a sickly, porcelain hue. His tawny eyes seem unfocused.

"How are you feeling?"

He smiles his charming smile. "Stiff and bruised, but I'll be fine."

"Are you sure? I think I should take you to the hospital. You don't *look* fine."

"Thanks a lot," he says. "I'm sure. Why would I need to go to a hospital? You are the most effective doctor anyone could ever have. Lay with me for a few minutes. That will make me feel better. And then I'll rest and let the ice set. By the way," he says, changing the subject, "Who was on the phone?"

I had forgotten about the phone call. "It was a wrong number. At least, that's what I told them. They were looking for a taxidermist."

"What?"

"Yeah, that's what I thought, too."

"Did it sound like it could be her?"

"From what Sophia said, I think it could have been her. But Sophia didn't give her our number."

Cameron groans and leans back against the corner of the sofa, resting his head back as he stares at the ceiling fan. "This is my fault."

I feel a microscopic twitch in my abdomen. "It could happen to anyone."

"No, it couldn't, Bishop. *We* aren't *anyone*. We're *us*, and this shouldn't be happening."

I sense a faint awareness, again, deep within my abdomen. A pinpoint of light, burning against the inner darkness.

"Okay, now that we've both done our blame game, let's try to just move forward and do what we need to do." I turn my sensors up on high, but his shield holds steady. The only time I see anything out of place is when I look at his face, his eyes. But he feels strong to me right now, so I decide not to push the issue of taking him to the hospital.

"How much did you get done?" I ask him.

His unearthly eyes focus on mine. "The roof is finished. I just sealed and finished securing the last rod right before I fell. What about you?"

"I finished up the entire front and the French doors, but the rest of the back still needs to be done. I have to go back out."

"Okay. I'm still alive and here if you need me." He pulls me against him again.

"Yeah, barely. I hope that I won't."

"When you're done, we need to go for a ride." His flannel shirt beneath my cheek smells of fresh spring air, sunshine, and cold mud.

"I'm not taking you. I'll go by myself."

"It's too much for you to do alone."

"In one day, sure." I look at him, taking in his pale face, his disheveled black curls, the bump on his head. I worry for him. For us.

Four

I spend the next hour shoring up the rest of the defenses on the outside of the house. When I am finished, I load the Jeep with the things I will need: more paint solution, paint brushes and a paint gun, the etcher, salt and salt spreader, shovel, the standard toolbox, and the first aid kit. Not that the meager first aid kit will really be helpful in the event of any life-threatening emergency.

It is 1:30 by the time I am slowly driving around the perimeter of the Wilson 27.

I am not sure whether there is enough daylight left to ride the entire fence line. If it had been the two of us together, it would have taken half the time. As it is it's only me, and how long it takes depends upon how much our wards have deteriorated throughout the winter, in addition to any material repairs that need to be done.

In the winter months, we check the fences less regularly than during spring through fall, when we ride the fences once a month and after severe storms. We perform major repairs when immediately necessary and maintenance work twice per year, in the fall and in the spring. I may not finish the work today, because it involves refreshing our wards. Maybe Cam will have srecovered a bit more by tomorrow, and will be able to help me finish up.

I don gloves and the particle mask to lessen the effects of the iron powder contained within the paint solution and the iron ward-posts that we have in place in addition to the standard wooden fence posts. My great-grandfather and a close circle of his friends forged each of them by hand, at the smithy that still stands on the 27.

Our property once hosted a veritable compound of families, making the Wilson 27 its own community, which eventually expanded out into the surrounding town. Aside from my family's taxidermy and the Tanners' tannery, there was a laundry, a bakery, the smithy, and the icehouse.

Before my forefathers emigrated from Scotland, they studied the many maps drawn by the most expert cartographers throughout the centuries since the New World had been discovered. They consulted the most trusted environmentalists, geologists, soothsayers, and oracles to identify a collective of ley lines that determined the location of their initial settlement. The paths and tracks had been heavily traversed and crossed in this location, and contained concentrations of energy that could be harnessed for usages both physical and metaphysical.

This convergence, appearing as it did in an ideal geographical setting of lush forest, fertile soils and fields, on the gentle slopes beside the crystal clear lake, made this particular spot valuable and desirable to my forefathers. Oddly enough, while there were other settlements dotted here and there throughout Upstate New York, the area now known as Wilson Lake was overlooked as a place of value – until my family settled here.

Many of the families that had once subscribed to the homesteading way of life subsequently embraced the modern delivery systems of energy and moved off of the 27 into the surrounding town. My family adamantly preserved the "natural" way of living life, and refused to allow wires and gas lines to encroach on the property – even more specifically, cable lines meant for communication. This played a large part in the dispersal of the families of the 27. They built new homes, established businesses, opened elementary and high schools. But the Wilson 27 was always the hub of the town, and still remains its axis.

Eventually, my father allowed the sparest of updates – electricity for the lighting, the telephone landline, and the cable television. We still use steam and wood heat. There are no gas lines on the property. The buildings that were once used are still maintained. The town's Historical Society takes care of them. And, in the event of an emergency, they can be put into operation at a moment's notice. If the grid goes down, the Wilson 27 is ready to go.

I park the Jeep several yards ahead and jog back to my starting point, then work my way forward to the Jeep, inspecting and spraying the posts as I go. I etch the sigils back into the iron where necessary and spread salt around the boundary with the salt spreader. I straighten tilted or loose fence posts, hammer them down securely, and make sure that all of the adjoining slats are also firmly attached. Once I reach the Jeep, I drive forward several more yards, and repeat.

All of our iron fence posts are etched with sigils and wards, fortified before being driven into the ground and fixed in concrete. All of these and the wooden fence posts are also painted with the metal and salt solution. One would think that salt would rust the iron, but the compound of our solution was carefully crafted to act as a protectant; and the frequency of repainting prevents oxidation from taking a firm grip.

We use salt because it is one of the greatest protective elements against evil known to mankind. We also have running water in the form of a diverted stream. My forefathers spent countless man-hours splitting the original stream, which runs from the north, so that the two resulting branches now run parallel on the east and west borders and join once again on the southern border, encircling the 27.

The running water performs double-duty; it contributes to the powering of our electricity and also serves as a shield against negative energy forces.

The perimeter of the Wilson acreage is a sight to see on a clear night beneath the full moon; and is even more awesome when it is completely overcast. I have had the opportunity to witness the aerial view on several occasions. The wards that we

STUFFED ANIMALS

have carved out glow bright blue through the darkness. The A-frame glows, as well. If you have ever wondered whether magic truly exists, you will know for sure if you ever fly over the Wilson 27 at night.

I hear loud footsteps and the sound of rustling foliage and snapping twigs and branches; the noise of something big approaching me through the woods. A huge figure emerges from the edge of the trees and lumbers toward me. Ursa Major – Major, for short – is a brown bear, mother of Ursa Minor, her now full-grown cub.

I found them both in the fall of 1985, after a wind shear had moved through the area, ripping up trees and causing all manner of destruction throughout the 27. Baby Minor was crying beside his young mother, who lay slowly dying, knocked unconscious by a blow from the large branch of a fallen elm tree. I knew that I didn't have a lot of time to play around; I needed to act fast.

Major remains my most successful revivication.

Pepper, my dad's fox companion, was my second most successful. I guess I may as well call him a "pet" – more aptly, a "wild" pet, or at least, as much of a pet as a wild animal can be.

My dad was a loner, though he had family and close friends. He kept to himself, for the most part, and spoke little, and what few words he used imparted wisdom. My mother had died when I was an infant, and he had never found another woman to accompany him through life.

Pepper had shown signs of aging, and my dad knew that the faithful fox would precede him to the grave. He asked me to revive Pepper when it was his time; he didn't say as much, but I knew it was because Pepper was all he had. He had me, but I was not the same. I love Pepper equally as much as my father did, and that was part of the reason I granted him his wish.

I have tried to be selective with the use of my gift. I had misgivings about Pepper. I should have refused my father's request. But I didn't, and now Pepper outlives him.

I wish I knew whether Major or Pepper experience the same quality of life as normal living creatures who had not been reanimated. Do they feel the same? They are capable of recognition, of bonding, of affection. They are not zombies; they don't show unwarranted aggression or bloodthirsty tendencies. I did not know Ursa Major before I revived her; but I feel that she is more friendly and docile than she may have been before the fact.

I don't know whether my use of my abilities is ethical. I would like to think that I have been given the gift for a purpose.

Before I die, I plan to release both Major and Pepper. The one most prominent effect of having been revived is immortality, and I am not sure how much of a gift that is, as the organic body breaks down. Does one grow tired and weary? Or do the mind, body, and soul all regenerate regularly when they begin to break down? Is there pain?

I talk to Major, scratch her behind her massive ears, and she wraps me in a giant, warm bear hug that engulfs me entirely. I wrinkle my nose at her strong, musky odor. She sits and watches as I move along the fence line, listening to my running commentary and occasionally throwing in a gesture, tapping me with her dinner plate-sized paw, or leaning gently against me. She doesn't make any noise, as her vocal chords haven't worked since I revived her. Pepper's don't, either.

I wonder why Jon the raven is still able to use his voice and Major and Pepper are not. Ravens are able to mimic voices. Maybe this has something to do with the difference.

When it is time to get back in the Jeep and move further down the fence line, Ursa trots along beside me.

Halfway around the property, I stop and stare.

"What the hell?"

There is a large trench on the other side of the fence, deep near the fence and growing shallower as it extends further away. It looks as though something has either tried to dig its way beneath the fence, or else something large hit the ground and slid toward the fence, creating a furrow. I visually search the tree line outside the fencing and the distance of green field between it and the fence, but I can see no sign of what may have caused the trench.

Major lumbers up to the fence rods and sniffs the earth around them. She shows her teeth in a silent snarl. Apparently she smells something she doesn't like.

I stand as close as possible to the fencing and inspect the ground just outside of the posts. The earth at the bottom and edges of the furrow are scorched, as is the grass on either side. The smell of ozone hangs in the air. I look down to the closest point of the trench, and I see that it stops abruptly when it reaches the fence. There are no signs of disturbance on the inside.

The scorched earth, the huge trench, the smell of ozone; these are all indicators of something that I haven't dealt with in years: fire magic. An attack.

I pass my gloved hand close to the fencing at the point of impact. The wards on the posts glow white-hot. They are undamaged and intact. The only effect of the incident is the angle of three of the closest fence posts, which have been knocked slightly askew. The attack was ineffective. If someone was searching for access to our property through magical means, they didn't get it.

This is also the furthest point from the house. Whatever it was that caused the trench hadn't wanted to attract attention; the impact would have been loud.

This happened recently. Maybe even this morning.

I think about Cameron's accident.

Are the two incidents related?

There is a twitch deep in my abdomen. The tiny spark of light begins to pulse; at least, that is how I picture it. Because that is how it feels.

A hot sweat breaks over me. My stomach begins turning. Weak at the knees, I make it to the Jeep and slump on the edge of the passenger seat. I lean forward and retch. I throw up fluorescent yellow bile onto the green grass.

Major comes over and quietly nuzzles me. My body trembling, I lean against her, grateful for her warm, solid presence. I remain there for a few moments, until the nausea has passed. Hunger gnaws at my stomach. I fumble in the glove box and pull out one of the protein bars I have stashed there. When my stomach has settled, I return to work.

I continue to push through with repairs until the sun is low in the sky. Major eventually lumbers away, back into the woods.

I make great headway with the perimeter, but I still haven't quite finished the job when I reach another blast point identical to the first.

Five

The sun begins its descent behind the horizon line. I still have a portion of the fencing to check, but I reluctantly give it up for the time being.

Back at the A-frame, Cam is looking better. He has made a small fire to dispel the night-time chill. The smell of his cooking wafts deliciously from the kitchen. My stomach growls greedily, but I am concerned that Cameron is up and moving around.

"You made dinner?"

He smiles at me from his spot in the corner of the sofa. "MacArthur Special."

"Oh, okay." A MacArthur Special is Cameron's homemade version of a frozen TV dinner. He pre-makes a few dinners every month, to save us time on busy nights – or when I have to make dinner. I am not known for my stellar culinary talents.

I plop down beside him on the sofa and he wraps his arms around me, gathering me in. I squeeze him gently and kiss him, then move away from him a little when I see him wincing.

"How is the fence line?" he asks.

I update him on my progress and tell him about the trenches.

His lips flatten into a thin line. "I should have gone with you. You could have been hurt."

"But I'm okay. The attack happened before I got there."

"What if it didn't?"

"There is no point in asking 'what if?'. I just wish I could have finished."

"If I had worn the harness, I wouldn't have had the stupid accident, and I could have gone with you, and you would have been safer, and we would have finished, together."

I have my doubts that he could have kept me safe from either of those blasts, had I been in the direct line of fire at the time they were executed. I am probably better at protecting myself than he is. But I don't say that.

"Even if you had been wearing the harness, you would have still been injured. Maybe you wouldn't have fallen as far, but you still would have been struck by the lightning bolt."

He takes my hand. After a moment, he groans as an expression of understanding crosses his face. "You're right. The lightning strike was no accident. It was a *diversion*. Or else, maybe the phone call was the diversion."

"So you are thinking the same thing I've been thinking. There wasn't just one attack. There were four simultaneous attacks. The phone call was part of it. Then the attack on you. And the two blasts at the fence line. They were all part of the same event."

"Yes. That's what I think."

"I don't believe it worked, though."

"Why? What do you think they wanted?"

"Unless they wanted you injured – which they *did* succeed at – they wanted access to the property. Other than that, I don't know."

"And you believe Elspeth Sinclair is behind all of this?"

"Yes. Elspeth Sinclair."

He falls silent. The flames crackle and jump.

"I don't think it is over, either," I say. "This took careful planning and an extreme amount of energy. It may be the beginning of something." The smell of food becomes overwhelming, and suddenly I feel lightheaded, nauseous, sick with hunger. "How long has the MacArthur Special been in the oven? It smells done."

He glances at the grandfather clock in the corner. "It *is* done. Would you mind doing the honors?"

"Sure. Would you like to eat in here?" He nods. "I'll bring it out, then."

In the kitchen, I shut the oven off and remove the glass casserole dish. My mouth waters and a painful hollow feeling contracts my stomach. The pinpoint Spark glows in its internal darkness.

I prepare two plates, a basket of bread, and pull Cameron's pre-made green salad out of the fridge. I poke my head out of the swinging door and see that Cameron has set up our television tray tables.

We dig in. This MacArthur Special is Cameron's signature chicken broccoli Alfredo

I love my husband.

After dinner, I clear the plates and pour some wine. We forego the furs and take our wine on the sofa in favor of Cameron's injuries.

The pinpoint Spark in my belly is a constant light. I am not sure what it means, but I am beginning to suspect, so I sip my wine sparingly.

I gradually become aware of a throbbing in my right hip, shoulder, and knee. There is a steady pain in my forehead. Random, foreign thoughts flit through my mind.

"Cam, are you feeling okay?" I ask.

"I've got a headache. And aches and pains in my body, from the fall. I don't think that it's anything to worry about, though. I think I'll be all right in a few days. Why?"

"I think you're leaking."

"What?"

"You are *leaking*. I am feeling the pains from your accident, and your thoughts are seeping out. I think your injuries are greater than you think."

"I'm just a little distracted with the aches and pains. I'll try to be more mindful."

"I think you should go to the hospital."

"Aw, let's give it the night, okay? You know an evening at the hospital is exhausting. I don't think either of us is in any kind of shape for that. I think that spending the night with you, in our own bed, will be the best remedy. You had to heal in an emergency on the fly today, and there hasn't been substantial

STUFFED ANIMALS

time. I think a night wrapped up with you will be all the healing I need."

I consider it. He may be right. I am an innate healer. The wounded often benefit simply from my presence. There are a lot of wounded people out there – that is why I prefer to maintain my solitude. The sheer volume of hurt in the world drains me and leaves me empty.

"Okay. We'll just hang and relax tonight, go to bed early. If you're up to it, we can finish the last few yards of fence line tomorrow. Then we'll take the rest of the day off. But if you are still having problems in a couple of days, would you at least go see Dr. Simms?"

He draws an "x" across his chest with his finger. "Cross my heart."

I draw Cam a hot bath, tossing in a couple capfuls of bubble bath. When the tub is ready, he eases himself back into the hot water with a prolonged exhalation of relief.

Afterward, I extinguish the flames in the lanterns that we habitually use in the bedroom, then slip between the sheets. His skin is warm; he smells of soap and sandalwood from the bath, his dark curls, still damp. I drape my arm across his bare chest and move so that my body presses comfortably against his, skin to skin, from shoulder to ankle.

He puts his arm around me and pulls me tightly to him. Beneath the moonlight that shines upon us through the skylight, he looks into my eyes. "I think it's working already. I'm feeling great!"

"I'm glad. You really scared me today. Don't do that again."

His shield is in place and working; there are no random thoughts, no distracting psychic trickles. He kisses my neck, my cheek, my forehead, my nose, my mouth. His kiss is long, slow, his lips, soft and warm.

"Good night, Vixen," he murmurs in the dimness.

"Good night, Mr. President," I whisper back.

Six

*W*e keep our eyes open for any further unusual incidents around the Wilson 27, touring the fences each weekend. But days grow into weeks that pass without incident.

The sleeping town of Wilson Lake is now fully awakened from the long winter, and spring activities are in full swing. As the temperatures rise and the days grow steadily warmer, soccer and baseball practices fill up the local elementary and high school sports fields on weeknights and weekends. The parks and playgrounds fill with picnickers and children every day after school, and the music of live bands can be heard floating through the evening air, emanating from the bandstand at Daniel Green, the main park situated on the hill that rises from the beach. On any given day, canoes, sailboats, and other water craft are in evidence on the sparkling waters of Wilson Lake.

My work shifts to a lot of big fish and waterfowl mounts. I still get plenty of river otters, foxes, coons, mink, and the like; but when the lake thaws, there is more opportunity for collectors to bag water creatures.

We harvest our kitchen garden regularly, and Cam maintains our fresh produce and canned-goods booth at the Wilson Lake Farmer's Market on Main Street every other Saturday.

STUFFED ANIMALS

He eagerly fires up the barbecue. His cold-weather menu shifts to spring and summer fare: chilled fruit, pasta and green salads; grilled fish, steak, chicken, vegetables; frozen desserts. Anything that can be marinated and grilled, he marinates and grills. He hones his bartending skills with all manner of mixed drinks – from most of which, I take only a small taste, pretending to drink them.

Where previously, I had thought the Spark to be an insignificant and temporary sensation – a bug, maybe – I have revised my opinion. For, instead of fading out and disappearing, it seems to have taken up permanent residence within my belly, growing in microscopic increments. It feels larger, brighter, and more tangible with the passing days. My monthly fails to arrive, and I begin to suspect that the Spark may be more than just a "Spark".

I still don't believe that early spring attacks are an isolated incident. It has only been about a month and a half, and I am still on my guard; but there is nothing to be seen. Somewhere in the back of my mind, I form the idea that the attackers have simply retreated to either develop a new plan, or they are waiting until the right time to execute the next phase.

Regardless, I am getting to the point where I need to tell Cameron about the Spark, and I prepare to do exactly that, this evening.

Our bellies full after another mouth-watering meal, Cam and I recline upon the furs. We are sufficiently warm not to need the actual fire, so we have a realistic screen set into the fireplace that gives the appearance of crackling flames, without the heat.

I can feel Cameron glancing at me; I can also feel his expectant energy charging the air. He is excited about something. I look at him, and he looks at the fire. The flames reflect in his eyes.

"Spit it out, already!" I say, exasperated.

"Okay. I have News!" he says, sounding delighted.

Oh, no. I don't like it when Cameron has "News". Whenever he makes this kind of announcement, my first reaction is to duck and cover. I try not to let my emotions show on my face. I wear what I like to think of as a neutral, but encouraging, smile.

"Okay?"

"Have I ever told you about my half-brother?"

"Yes. You've mentioned him, briefly. But according to you, there wasn't much to tell. He died at birth."

"That's what *I* thought!" Cameron smiles widely. "But it wasn't true! He is alive and well! And I am going to meet him!"

I freeze, feeling the hairs stand up on the back of my neck. I don't want to be a spoilsport, but experience has given me reason to use caution, and suspicion comes to me naturally. I choose my words with care.

"Tell me."

He proffers a piece of paper, seemingly from nowhere, and hands it to me. I unfold it. It is a handwritten letter. I look at him with raised eyebrows. Still grinning, he gestures. "Read it!"

I move closer to the flames to read the neat handwriting, penned with black ink. The letter is from one Quinlan Winter, purporting to be Cameron's half-brother and requesting that the two of them meet.

After I finish reading the letter, I pretend that I am still reading it, trying to buy some time and gather my thoughts. I feel skeptical; but just because I have misgivings about the letter, it doesn't mean that author and the contents aren't genuine, so I try to adopt a calm and encouraging, yet diplomatic attitude.

"So are you going to meet him?"

"Of course! I may have a sibling out there! Or at least, a *half*-sibling," he corrects himself.

"You 'may'? You mean you aren't sure whether you believe him?"

"I'm just trying to keep an open mind. My first reaction was suspicion and disbelief. But, as you and I both know, life is messy. Things happen. I figure I could at least meet the guy, check him out, see if he seems legit."

I nod once. "Okay, that's logical. Vet him, find out for sure. You must be excited. I mean, with the prospect of a long-lost brother, and all."

"I am! It would be awesome to discover that I have a brother, for real!"

"So… when does this big rendezvous take place?"

"Lunch, tomorrow."

"Oh, not wasting time."

"Why would I?"

"Indeed, why would you?"

"Well, he's staying at a hotel in Jermanic River. He made the trip here just for this purpose. I don't want him to spend more money than he has to for room and board." He suddenly looks apprehensive. "What do *you* think about this, Vixen? You aren't saying a lot."

"I'm reserving judgment. I don't have enough information to say anything. I think this is something that *you* need to investigate. Do I feel that it's odd that he showed up on the heels of some weird incidents? Sure. But just like you, I want to keep an open mind. Go find out what's what. I think this could be an awesome thing for you, but I also don't want you to be disappointed if it doesn't turn out like you hope."

Cameron scooches close and wraps his arms around me. I can feel how content he is; and his excitement is pouring out of him, tempered slightly by the wine. "If Quinlan Winter disappoints me, I still have you to come home to. You could take the sting out of any kind of disappointment."

I lean my head on his shoulder and sink into his warmth.

Now is not the time to tell him about the Spark.

* * *

The next day, Cameron's face is lit with an inner light as he prepares to meet his half-brother. I like how he looks when he is this happy. I am glad he looks like this often, and isn't just his lunch with Quinlan Winter that puts this kind of smile on my husband's face and brings his glowing energy out.

Before he leaves, he slides the canoe into the back of the Jeep for me. I have my own plans to enjoy while he is at his reunion lunch.

I say goodbye to him next to the open door of his Versa Note. His kiss is long and sensual. Always.

"Have fun!" I tell him. "See you in a while!"

"I love you, Vixen!"

"I love you back, Mr. President."

He smiles his sunlit smile and folds himself into the driver seat. He waves before pulling down the long gravel drive. I wave back.

All is calm; all is right.

I am nervous about this Quinlan Winter, but most of the unsettled feeling comes from the Spark, who is pulsing brightly in my belly. I push my anxiety aside and drive the Jeep down to Wilson Lake, upon whose surface I am eager to take my first voyage of the season. The pond on the 27 is okay, and offers a closer canoeing site; but today I hunger for bigger water. The wide open waters of Wilson Lake call to me, their surface gently breeze-rippled and glittering like billions of diamonds beneath the summer sun.

I back the Jeep down to edge of the launch and carefully pull the craft from the rear and maneuver it into the water. I paddle to one of my favorite, less-frequented shores and spend the afternoon with the Spark, who soon calms, along with my rolling stomach. I sit against the trunk of a willow tree that has an indentation just large enough for me to recline back into comfortably, with the help of a pillow I tucked into the canoe. I open my book and immerse myself in a fantasy story, the air warm upon my legs and the ripe, green grass soft beneath my feet and between my toes.

* * *

When I return to the A-frame, Cameron is there before me, riding around on the lawn mower. He sees me and his face lights up. He holds up his index finger, a signal for me to hold on a moment.

I sit at the picnic table on the back deck while he stows the mower in the shed.

He settles beside me and greets me with a kiss. His normally pale face is red from sun and the heat.

"Weeellll?" I ask

"Well, what?" he responds.

I roll my eyes and shove him lightly on the shoulder. "*You know what!* Is he legit?"

His tawny eyes are wide with excitement, but I don't even need to look at him to feel how elated he is. Joy radiates from him in waves. "He *looks* legit. You wouldn't *believe* how legit he looks."

"You mean he looks like you?"

STUFFED ANIMALS

"Yeah, and that is an understatement. He is nearly identical."
"Really? But I thought he was your 'half'."
"He *is* my 'half'. But he looks more like an identical."
"For real?"
"For real."
"Where did you go to eat?"

Cameron sits with his back against the table, stretching his long, denim-clad legs out in front of him. "Georgie's, where else?"

"Oh, great choice!" Georgie's is Wilson Lake's best casual family diner on the waterfront.

"It was packed."

"I'll bet, on a nice Saturday like this. And how did you and baby bro get along? Do you guys have much in common?"

"Other than our looks, we're pretty different. We had a lot to talk about, though, starting with what happened when he was born."

"Oh, yeah? That must have been quite the discussion. What *did* happen?"

His expression grows serious. "My dad paid off his mother so that she would take Quinlan, disappear, and stay quiet. He didn't want a scandal. More specifically, he didn't want my mother to know he'd had an affair."

"And let me guess: he doesn't have proof, either."

"Of what? Bishop!"

"Hold on, hold on! I'm not asking because of my suspicion, though I do think we should keep in mind all possibilities as to why he showed up. I *am* suspicious, though probably not for the reason you might be thinking. I am just saying, he has no way to prove his birthright, does he?"

"I don't know. I don't know what it says on his birth certificate, as far as paternity. But even so…"

I feel Cameron's mood drop.

"I'm angry," he says. "I'm disappointed, sad, and disillusioned. Because of my father's dishonesty, I missed a lifetime with my brother. And I am not even going to address what he did to my mother. I thought my dad was better than that."

I look down at my knees. "I'm sorry."

"Don't be. It had nothing to do with you." He shrugs. "We talked about a lot of stuff. Lunch seemed kind of short, actually. How do you cover nearly thirty-seven years in an hour and a half?"

"Why didn't you take longer?"

"He had to go. We're going fishing tomorrow, though, so we can catch up a bit more."

"Well, that's good! So what do you think about all of this?"

He smiles and drapes his arm across my shoulders. "I have mixed emotions about my dad. I'm sure I'll get over it and move on. The past is the past. But I'm glad to have met Quinlan. I'm happy he looked me up."

"If you're happy, I'm happy. " I wrap my arms around him. He smells of sunshine, ripe, freshly cut grass, and sweat.

"What about you, Vix? How was your afternoon of solitude?"

"Relaxing as hell."

"Just what you needed."

I smile. "You got that right. It's good for the soul." I lean against him, resting my head in the cradle of his neck and shoulder. We sit for a while, listening to the birds calling in the nearby woods, taking in the view of the field that stretches from the back yard to the tree line. The insect orchestra hums and buzzes beneath the summer sky.

I find myself on the edge of a doze, lulled by nature's music, the warmth of the day, and the feel of my husband's body against mine.

These are moments that I collect in the jar of my memory, adding to the ones I already have, to pull out and savor. These are moments of perfection. Perfect happiness. Perfect love. Utter contentment. A life that could never get any better, because it is already the best.

I should know that I already have too many of these moments saved up. From waking up beside Cameron to the sound of rain pattering on the skylight; lounging on the furs with our wine after enjoying succulent dinners he has prepared, or during winter evenings while the snow piles up outside, when our dancing fires keep us warm. The hugs, the kisses, the sharing of our personal worlds between the sheets.

STUFFED ANIMALS

I debate telling Cam about the Spark. I want him to know. I yearn to divulge my secret. The Spark grows and glows brighter with every passing day, and reaches for her father when he is near. I suspect that she shares his powers. She senses his presence and hears his voice mingling with mine. She recognizes that he and she are a part of one another.

Yes, I have begun to think of her as "she". I have a strong conviction that the Spark is female. A tiny seed of a girl.

Despite my urge to tell Cameron, I don't feel secure in telling him, now that Quinlan Winter has arrived on the scene. I have an inkling that he might have something to do with the attack in the early spring, only a couple of months past. An underlying anxiety that the attack was part of something that may have just begun, waiting to unfold, keeps me silent.

I don't know Quinlan Winter. My husband doesn't know him, either, despite his hopes and his willingness to accept this stranger with blind faith. My suspicious nature, handed down through my family's paternal bloodline, is what it is. I have no reason to believe that Quinlan has a hidden agenda or ulterior motive.

But I have no reason to believe that he doesn't.

I hear a *tap-tap-tap* on the wooden steps, and open my eyes to see Pepper sitting at my feet.

"Hey, Pep!" I reach out and stroke his fur, a faded red shot through with gray. He lifts his head, his snout aimed upward, his toothy, triangular mouth open in a wide smile.

Cameron regards me and the fox. "Two of a kind, you guys are. Red and red. Except one alive, the other, dead."

I roll my eyes and shoot him a look. He doesn't care much for what he considers the "darker" side of my talents, even though I have tried to explain to him that my resurrections are not really resurrections; that my patients haven't "died" in the true sense of the word. But I think the reality of this part of my gift scares him.

I can't help the gifts I have been given. What can I do except to use them? I could use them for a much different purpose.

As though the ability to influence others with his thoughts and emotions isn't a terrifying gift. At least, I feel that it would be, to the unwitting receiver of that influence – if only they knew.

He stretches languidly, squeezes me to him, kisses me. "I'm going to start putting dinner together." He unfolds himself from the picnic bench and disappears through the French doors.

I remain seated, unwilling to waste even a few moments of this idyllic summer day. Pepper rests his chin on my knee and I pet his sun-warmed fur, over and over.

Seven

Cameron's stubble scratches my cheek as he kisses me goodbye. I struggle to open my sleep-laden eyes and, through the skylight, I see a solid gray cloud bank. Dawn hasn't yet broken, and I am pretty sure that the sun won't be smiling down upon us today. As though in answer to my thoughts, tiny drops of moisture begin to tap gently on the skylight.

"Happy fishing," I tell him. "I love you, Mr. President."

"Go back to sleep," he whispers. "It's only five-thirty. I'll be back in a few hours. And don't worry about the chickens."

The bed shifts as he gets up. On his way out of the darkened doorway, he turns and says, "I love you back Vixen." I hear the smile in his voice.

Then he is gone, his footsteps descending the stairs.

I turn over, rolling onto his side of the bed. I bury my face in his pillows, inhaling deeply. It smells uniquely of Cameron, along with a hint of Drakkar and sweat. The smell comforts me, and I wrap the sheet and blanket around me against the morning chill. The rain starts to fall faster, and the sound on the skylight lulls me back down into sleep.

I wake to the same sound two hours later, with Jubilee Joe crowing in the background. I pull on my robe and wander downstairs to the kitchen. I flip on the light switch, instantly brightening the kitchen and the morning. I start a new pot of coffee.

Cameron has left me a gourmet breakfast sandwich in the fridge. Ever the culinary diva, "Oven Only, Do Not Microwave", he has written on the wax paper wrapper. I smile, preheat the oven, and pop the sandwich in for ten minutes.

I check the front porch and find the Sunday paper lying there, trussed up in a plastic bag to keep it dry. I sit at the table and through the French doors, watch the rain fall outside, drink my coffee, eat my sandwich, and read the paper.

The Spark begins to throb. With each pulse, she grows brighter and brighter. My skin prickles with goose bumps. A sweat slick breaks out over my entire body.

Nausea is upon me, and I run for the bathroom.

It is not my first bout of morning sickness. It usually hits me in the wee hours of the morning, when the A-frame is quiet except for the sound of Cameron's even breathing. I often find myself hurrying to the bathroom, then pulling the box of unsalted crackers out of the cupboard ten minutes later. I had been hoping to be one of the mothers that remain unaffected, but no such luck. I am surprised that Cameron hasn't noticed. At least, he hasn't said anything about it.

Today would mark between six and eight weeks.

I won't be able to hide the Spark from him for much longer. I need to start seeing a doctor. I may be a healer, but in the field of obstetrics, I am completely ignorant. I need to start educating myself about pregnancy, birth, and parenthood.

In the early days, the Spark had seemed just a dream. Now it hits home just how real she is.

After the shakes calm and the nausea subsides, I check the time and see that it isn't even nine o'clock. The rain taps steadily on the roof. The thought crosses my mind that it is great fishing weather.

I gather myself together, shower, and brush my teeth. I throw on a sweat suit, shove my feet into my rain boots, and shrug into my slicker. I slide into the front seat of the Jeep.

Stuffed Animals is closed Sundays, so I have the storefront to myself. The bell tinkles as I unlock the door and let myself in. The interior is shadowed and gloomy. My animals seem to look at me with recognition in their eyes. Many people would be creeped out by them, I guess. But my relationship with them is different, so it doesn't bother me.

I switch on the desk lamp in the office and boot up the laptop. I look up local obstetricians and write down a few names that I can call during the week. Dr. Simms has been our family doctor forever, but he is a general practitioner. Despite the fact that he is familiar with our family's traits, I feel that I will be more comfortable with a female obstetrician.

I go to Alibris and search pregnancy books. Then I look up lifestyle and dietary recommendations and what to do about morning sickness. I print out a couple of pages to take with me, then shut the laptop off.

As I am locking up, I become aware of the yawning emptiness in my stomach. The brightness that waxes and wanes inside my abdomen is almost like a sound. The nausea returns. I need food, fast.

I had planned on hitting the grocery store before I go home, but my body is insistent. I figure that Georgie's is the best way to go. As I swing the Jeep into the parking lot, I see Cameron's Versa Note parked in the front row of spaces outside of the restaurant.

As I open the door and walk into the diner, a chill crawls down my spine and my neck hairs stand at attention. Something feels wrong.

My shield goes up, my wall is in place.

They are at the counter, my husband and Quinlan Winter. Except for the clothing, I can't tell the difference between them from behind. Two guys with the same build, same height, same heads of curly, midnight black hair.

Georgie nods from the doorway into the kitchen. "How goes it, Mrs. MacArthur?"

"Great, Georgie!" I pull off my wet slicker and hang it on the wooden coat rack beside the door.

Cameron and his half-brother turn to look at me: two identical heads turn in tandem, revealing identical faces. But Quinlan's eyes are brown, not yellow topaz, like Cameron's. As I look a little longer, I see that Quinlan is slightly thicker, a little heavier, than Cam.

"Hey, Vix! What's going on?" I lean down and kiss my husband. "Bishop, meet my long lost brother, Quinlan Winter. Quinn, this is my lovely wife, Bishop."

I smile at Quinlan, who takes my offered hand and raises it to his lips. "Very pleased to meet you," he says. As soon as his hand touches mine, all of the hairs on my arm stand up, as though in the presence of a static electric field. My guards immediately slam into place and I mute my sudden fear: he is a transmitter.

"The same," I respond.

"What are you doing out here in this weather?" Cameron puts his arm around me, rubbing my back as I seat myself on the stool beside his. I lean into his warmth.

"Oh, I had a couple of things to check at the shop, and I didn't realize how hungry I was, so I stopped in for a bite. Speaking of 'bites', how about you guys? Did you catch anything?"

"Yep!" Cam beams. "We did, actually. Quinn caught a nice one." Quinn nods in agreement, his smile a close match with my husband's.

I order some lunch while Cameron and his brother engage in conversation.

I sit quietly as I wait for my open-faced turkey sandwich, listening and breathing deeply, trying to calm the Spark and my growing nausea. I am still on my guard, my shield well in place against the curious sensors that reach out to test me.

I can feel that Quinlan's skill is much more honed than Cameron's – and possibly more powerful. I force my interior demeanor to stay steady and non-committal, giving away nothing more than the pleased surprise of meeting my husband. I keep my wariness tucked under a veil, because who knows whether Cam's half-brother has additional "gifts"?

Cameron, however, seems oblivious to Quinlan's power. He is a more trusting soul than I am, and this is his long-lost brother, after all, something he has been yearning for since he was a child. But Cam's apparent lack of awareness about Quinn's power bothers me. I hope that he has used discretion in what information he has disclosed. I am now firmly convinced that revealing the Spark's existence to Cam any time soon would be a mistake.

I don't have to talk much, as Georgie is quick and soon sets my plate in front of me. I begin eating my lunch as Cameron and Quinn finish theirs. They sit and talk afterward, and I know that Cameron is hanging around to be courteous to me, waiting until I am finished with my meal before he tells me goodbye.

I down my food in silence, savoring the hot turkey bathed in creamy gravy and the crisp, salty French fries that warm me against the dampness and clouds of the gloomy, rainy day. Relief washes through me as the sustenance quells my nausea and calms the Spark a bit.

After I have cleaned my plate, Cameron says, "We're going to head out. I'm going to get Quinn back to the hotel, and then I've got a couple of fish to clean." He kisses me.

"I'm going to stop at the grocery store and grab a few things before I come home. I'll see you in a little bit."

"It was good to meet you, half-sister-in-law," Quinn says.

"Likewise, Quinn," I respond. "Congratulations on your catch today."

He gives me a smile that has something behind it that I don't know how to define.

They head out the door into the rain. I watch through the window as Cam's Note pulls out of the parking lot.

The alarm bells in my mind quiet as the distance grows between me and Quinlan Winter, but I am left unsettled.

* * *

I've been curled up beneath a warm blanket in my favorite reading chair in our small library alcove, but I've finished my book. I stand up to shelve it and begin looking for my next read when I sense something behind me.

I turn to see Quinlan Winter standing a mere few inches away. His eyes are closed as he exhales deeply. Apparently I've caught him sniffing my hair.

He smiles. "Hello, green-eyed lady," he says.

Hey, hon!" Cameron calls as he pushes through the door from the kitchen.

I take an involuntary step back, away from Quinn, and my shoulders meet the bookshelf.

Cam smiles his easy smile.. "I hope you don't mind a dinner guest tonight. I felt guilty about leaving Quinn at the hotel alone and invited him to dine with us."

I swallow my disappointment and force a bright smile. "No not at all. What do you plan on making?"

"Lemon pepper fish and herbed summer squash."

My stomach lurches. "That sounds really good, but I may have to pass on the fish. I'm still full from lunch."

"That's okay. I'm not cooking for a couple of hours yet. It's still early."

"I've been feeling a bit rough today. I think I'll go lie down."

Cameron's expression changes to one of concern. He stands and places a palm against my forehead. "Are you feverish?"

I shake my head. "I don't think so."

I catch a look at Quinlan. He is staring at my belly. Just then, he looks up and catches my eye. And, just for a split second, his mouth forms a smirk. Then it is gone, and I am not sure if I even saw it.

Cameron pulls a glass from the cupboard and fills it with ice water. "Why don't you go up and rest? I can bring you some chicken and rice a little later. We'll just hang and shoot the breeze." He gives me the glass, and as his fingers brush mine a soothing sensation spreads through my hand and runs up my arm, then washes down into my body. I know he is trying to help me feel better.

"That sounds good, thank you, Cam." I look at Quinn apologetically. "I'm sorry to be a downer of a host."

He shakes his head emphatically. "Not to worry! I'm sorry to see that you aren't feeling well. I hope I'll see you when you feel better."

His dark brown eyes look at me from the likeness of my husband's face. They are fathomless and curious, and I try not to meet them for too long, not knowing his level of perception.

I turn and head up the stairs to the loft. I pile the pillows behind me on the bed, pull the quilt over me, and sip my water. I set the glass down on the bedside table and recline, closing my eyes.

STUFFED ANIMALS

I take inventory of how I feel, physically. My stomach is calm right now, still comfortably full from Georgie's. The Spark is calm, as well; I sense she is tired. I think the nausea and vomiting have worn her out as much as it has exhausted me.

If this is how just one day at six weeks pregnant feels, I fear we are in for a long, tough ride.

I breathe deeply. Keeping my guard up, I extend my senses beyond the room. I hear the television switch on, and I know that the two men have moved into the living room, closer to the loft stairs.

Their presences are separate, but similar. Cameron's energy is light and easy. Quinlan's is a little heavier.

And I can feel it questing. Intent coupled with curiosity, spreading out, up the stairs, over the loft threshold.

I concentrate on remaining calm and centered, focused on shielding myself and the Spark. I whisper a few words, repeating the mantra six times, and pull the energy up around the bed, smoothing and coming together over my head like a dome. I feel it snap into place and seal.

Quinn's questing stops, abruptly cut off. I sense his energy hovering outside the loft threshold; then it slowly recedes.

He is talented and powerful. And I don't know who he is.

* * *

"Bishop," a voice whispers. I ascend from the depths of sleep. "Hey, are you awake?"

"Hey," I mumble. "What's going on?"

"Why are you sleeping in a bubble?"

"Because it helps me feel better."

"How *are* you feeling?" Cam's cool hand smoothes my hair back from my forehead.

"Why did you wake me up?"

"I'm taking Quinn back to Jermanic River. I just didn't want you to wake to an empty house without knowing where I've gone."

"Did you guys eat?"

"Yeah. I brought you food earlier, but I didn't want to wake you. If you feel hungry, your plate is in the fridge."

"You're too good to me, Mr. President."

"That's because I love you so much, my copper-haired minx." He gently nuzzles my neck. He smells like beer.

"How much have you had to drink? Are you sure I shouldn't drive you?"

"I only had two. I'll be fine. I'm sure I'm plenty under the limit."

"I hope so. I don't want to have to bail you out or pay you a visit in the hospital."

"Don't talk like that."

"Just come back safe and sound."

"I will." His lips are soft and warm on mine. "I'll see you soon, Vixen."

His footsteps recede down the stairs. He and Quinn exchange brief words. The front door closes; the Note starts up.

I am now fully awake. My head throbs and my stomach feels like a cavern, painfully empty. I drag myself downstairs. Food and a painkiller will help.

Some of the brief reading that I did online at Stuffed Animals informed me that acetaminophen is safe to take in moderation during pregnancy. I rummage for some in the bathroom cabinet and read the date on the bottle. I swallow two and wash them down with water.

The kitchen smells faintly of pan-fried fish. My tummy rolls a little, but I stay at the kitchen table while I wait for the microwave beeps to let me know that my chicken and rice are ready.

I tuck my feet under me on the sofa in the dimly lit living room and eat slowly. It is a wonder that even bland food like chicken and rice are so delicious when Cameron makes it. I can't help but wonder if he can actually transmit flavor into foods the way that he can transmit emotions into people.

I take it easy, not wanting to over-fill my stomach, and set my plate aside on the coffee table before it is empty. The food has helped my headache recede a little. I lie back on the sofa and breathe, knowing that deep, calm breathing will help both my headache and my digestion.

I am big on breathing. It works for almost every ailment, including illnesses and anxious thoughts.

STUFFED ANIMALS

I feel the Spark gradually pulse more brightly; a moment later, I hear tires crunching on gravel outside. The Spark's reaction tells me it is Cameron, returned from Jermanic River.

The front door closes firmly; the sound of Cameron's keys jingling as he hangs them on the hook beside the door. The kitchen door swings open and my husband brings the smell of fresh, damp air in with him. He bends over me, kisses me.

So many kisses. Cameron is always kissing me. Good mornings, good nights, hellos, goodbyes, periods of time and the conversations in between are punctuated with kisses. If Cameron had a nickel for every time kisses me, he could retire early.

But he has never given me a perfunctory kiss, whether on the cheek, forehead, hand, or lips. There is never just a "peck". Every single kiss he has given me conveys meaning, and tells me, in no uncertain terms, how much he loves me.

Cameron sits beside me on the sofa, pulling my legs across his lap.

"And how is Mrs. MacArthur feeling now?"

"I'm starting to feel a bit better. Thank you for asking, Mr. MacArthur."

He rubs my legs for a few minutes, then stretches his body alongside mine, positioning himself so that my head rests against his shoulder.

We lay together, his warmth bleeding into me. Serenity rolls thorough me. It travels from my stomach to my heart to my head. I can almost feel the blood vessels in my head contract, the pressure pulling back from my sinuses, the swelling in my brain going down.

"Thank you," I tell him.

"You're welcome," he whispers.

His warmth is golden, like sunlight, and it envelopes me in safety and security. Eventually, I doze. I feel Cameron reach up and over me as he pulls the afghan from the back of the sofa to cover us both.

Eight

I smell bacon and coffee.

I yawn and stretch in the morning sunshine that streams into the A-frame through the living room windows, and realize that I have spent the entire night on the sofa.

I schlep through the swinging door into the kitchen, and Cameron, dressed in his customary gray t-shirt, flannel pajama bottoms, and frilly white apron, sets a mug of coffee on the table. I seat myself and add cream and sugar. Moments later, a plate of scrambled eggs, bacon, and toast appears before me. The Spark protests loudly and my stomach turns with hunger. I grab a slice of toast and begin to gobble it down.

"It looks like you've recovered," Cameron says, sitting opposite me.

"Maybe," I say. "I think it's too early to tell."

He gives me a quiet, considering look before he begins to pile the fluffy yellow eggs onto a slice of his toast. He folds it in half and takes a big bite.

I try to slow down, but it is difficult to pace my eating when my stomach has once again become a yawning cave.

Cameron pauses after finishing his first egg sandwich half. "Bishop, do you ever regret having been placed in an arranged marriage with me?

STUFFED ANIMALS

I set my fork down on my plate and look at him. I slowly and deliberately finish chewing. "Why would you ask me such a thing?" I don't know whether I should feel amused or angry. What I do feel is shocked that after spending basically our entire lives together, that he would even be thinking about this.

He has been looking at me, his tawny eyes searching my face. Now he looks down and away beneath the weight of my stare. He shrugs one shoulder as though suddenly bashful, or ashamed of having asked. "I don't know. Sometimes I wonder whether you are really happy."

I push my plate away. My appetite is gone. "Have you *seen* me, Cameron? Have you *looked* at me, since we have been married? Have I ever given you a reason to wonder that?"

He refuses to meet my eyes. "I guess not."

"Then why ask? Where did you get such an idea?"

"I just wondered that because you never had a chance to – to try dating other guys. You didn't have the option to see whether you might like someone else better. To decide if I was really the one for you." He looks up at me. His expression is one of helplessness, like he knows he has just made a mistake, but he can't unmake it now, and he has to deal with the consequences.

I push back the end of the bench seat upon which I have been sitting. The feet scrape across the wooden planking. I stand up and look at my husband, wondering whether my own expression conveys the coldness that I feel chilling my heart.

"I have never felt that I was deprived of options or denied a choice. If you believe for one second that you were my only lot in life because it was decided for me, you are dead wrong. I have *always* had a choice. I have *always* had the option of walking away from you. I *chose* not to. My father would *never* have forced me to marry against my wishes. Don't be deluded into thinking that I would always have been *yours*, regardless of my own feelings."

"Bishop, wait! I didn't mean-"

I am already upstairs, in the loft. I pull on a pair of loose shorts, a tank top, and socks.

Cameron is waiting for me at the bottom of the stairs. I push past him, and he follows me through the swinging door into the kitchen, where I sit on the bench and pull on my sneakers.

"Where are you going?"

"Out. Away from you."

"I'm sorry, I'm sorry! Can't we talk about this?"

"I don't feel like talking right now, so I'm not going to. It is my *choice* to disengage from this conversation."

"I didn't mean it that way!"

"Oh, you didn't?" The more he pushes it, the angrier I feel. A red tint colors my vision and my blood feels like it is boiling. "You didn't mean to be so arrogant as to believe that I could not have gone my own way, without you? Or that I could have chosen another suitor?"

"No. I mean, isn't that what an arranged marriage is?"

"You nitwit, we have been friends since we were babies! We were inseparable all throughout our childhoods! We were best friends! I loved you! If I had loved someone else, I would have married someone else, parents be damned!"

I slam the door behind me and storm into the early autumn. It is far too pleasant a day for me to feel this horrible. I am seething with rage that Cameron would think that I was his property. If that is his mentality, then what about our love? What about mine? Did that not matter to him? Would he still have wanted to marry me, had I not loved him?

Or would he have expected it, anyway, as his "right"? Did he marry me out of a sense of entitlement? What of all of the years of telling me the loved me? Has this always been a lie?

For a brief second, I consider taking off in the Jeep. I decide against it. I am too angry and I can't even see straight. I head into the quiet shadows of the woods.

The Spark emits only a mild glow, as though she has retreated into a hidden haven deep within, safe from my anger.

I sprint through the woods, keeping to a dirt path that I use often for morning runs. While I usually jog at a nice brisk pace, I don't often go charging full tilt. Today, though, the level of my rage is too much for me, and I need to discharge it. Maybe I can sweat it out like poison, and it will evaporate into the warm morning air.

I run as fast and as hard and as long as I can before a stitch in my side forces me to slow. I lean against a tree trunk, place both my palms against the bark, and lean my forehead against the rough, dry, uneven surface. I feel the tree's energy hum against my skin. Like the Spark, the sensation is like a sound.

Tear flow down my cheeks. Why am I so angry? Where has all of this anguish come from? This seems like far too petty of an issue for me to experience such a strong reaction.

Is Cameron right? Do I resent being married to him?

I had never thought so. I have always adored him. And my father talked with me prior to the marriage, more than once. A secret between the two of us, he had reiterated that the "arrangement" was for show, only. The final decision was to be mine. He told me that should I change my mind about marrying Cameron, that he would stand behind me and support the decision.

Though our families were close, I always sensed that my father didn't really approve of Cam. I suspect that my father may have hoped that I would back out of the marriage.

Cameron is wrong to assume that I had not been exposed to other men. I had dated when I was in my late teens and early twenties, as had he. He must never have realized that I had a social life outside of my relationship with him. Had he really been that oblivious? He must have thought that while he was away at boarding school that I sat there alone the whole time, pining over him.

How could he not have known?

I shake my head.

The pain in my side has faded, and I walk on.

Maybe all of this negative emotion is from my pregnancy. Maybe all of the physical changes have caused my hormones to derail.

The Spark glows softly, as though she has dared to peek around the curtain out the window after a storm has passed.

I walk to the old icehouse. Unlike most of the buildings on the grounds, it is constructed of stone. It is an unusual structure in that it is built over one of the many streams that crisscross the 27.

When in active use, the icehouse was located too far away from the lake for traditional ice harvesting and transport. Although the pond was available, as were horse-drawn wagons to haul the ice, my forefathers had discovered that it was more convenient to build the storage structure directly over the source of the ice, itself. When the cold season began, they would pull water up out of the creek in large molds not unlike giant versions of the ice trays that we use in household freezers to make ice cubes – that is, unless the household in question has a refrigerator with a built-in icemaker. When the temperatures dropped at night, the water would freeze in the molds, and they would hammer the bottoms to loosen the ice bricks, which were then stacked against the walls. This would continue until the stream froze; then, pickaxes were used to break the stream ice, and that was harvested, as well.

The icehouse is located in the heavily wooded center of the Wilson 27. This helps the structure to stay cool in the summer. In pagan and druidic circles, this center lies directly over the intersection of several ley lines, and is said to be one of the most powerful geographic locations in New York State. The high vibrational energy that emanates in this area is believed to accelerate healing and contribute to abundant crop growth and livestock health and longevity. It is an energy that has been called upon for many different purposes. My family and the surrounding community have thrived in this location.

This is one of the various reasons that, periodically, power hunters attempt to take possession of the land. Because the people of the region also manifest special abilities, they are often targeted, as well; resulting in abductions and other thefts by those outside our community who discover our secrets. So when people leave Wilson Lake to pursue lives elsewhere, they don't speak too openly about where they come from, and we try to remain as autonomous as we can. Given our history as a close-knit community, it isn't difficult.

Developers have attempted to come in and buy local land, but no one sells.

Depending upon my mood, I often visit the unused buildings that dot the 27. They each exude a different energy. The atmosphere within the icehouse is exceedingly calming. Surrounded as it is by trees, with its additional feature of on-premises organic running water, it is the most emotionally and spiritually safe structure on the property.

STUFFED ANIMALS

The icehouse is empty, save stacks of antique molds against the walls and rough-hewn stone benches. Years ago I brought thick cushions to top these.

The portion of the floor beneath which the stream runs is covered by a wooden lid. I kneel down and shove it to the side. I remove my socks and sneakers, drop one of the cushions at the edge of the floor, sit down and immerse my feet.

As I sit with my feet dangling in the gently running water, I empty my mind. I need cleansing from my anger, emptying of all of the poisonous emotions. After a few moments I begin to calm. My heart rate returns to normal.

I realize that it has been weeks since I've had any meaningful conversation with anyone other than Cameron. I have been isolating myself, and though I value my solitude, I am aware that a body and mind need a change of scenery, social interaction.

After about an hour, I feel centered enough to return to the A-frame. Cameron's Note is still in the driveway, but he is not the person I wish to see or talk to. I enter long enough to grab my wallet and keys located on the shelf just inside the kitchen door. Cameron is not in evidence, but I hear the shower running.

I jump in the Jeep and head down to Main Street.

My resident mounts look out at me through the plate glass windows as I exit the Jeep in front of Stuffed Animals. They welcome me with curious and friendly expressions. I notice several empty spots that had recently housed commissioned mounts. The bell above the door tinkles unobtrusively as I enter.

I hear the desk chair roll, and Sophia's thick black hair swings back as she cranes her neck to peek around the office doorway. A smile spreads across her face.

"Hey, Bish!" she says; then her head disappears and I hear the sound of the chair rolling back to its place in front of the desk.

"Hey Soph, how's it going?" I ask, rounding the edge of the doorway. I drop my wallet on the small table and pour myself a cup of coffee from the pot she has brewed. A vinyl record plays on the turntable that she keeps there; her choice today is blues, which plays softly in the background and soothes my mood.

"It's going well. All of your recent clients have picked up their mounts, and no balances are left outstanding."

"That's terrific! Any comments on the work?"

"Blake and Terrez are pleased as punch. Janus Finch nitpicked a little, but I could tell she really liked her mount."

"That's so good to hear! I'm glad they're happy." I pull out one of our metal chairs and sit down, letting out a relieved breath. It feels good to be away from the new oppressiveness of the A-frame and in Sophia's pleasant, good-natured energy

"*And* you have an influx of new work." She hands me a stack of work orders.

I rifle through them, counting. "I guess! *Nine?* Nothing but good news, here!"

"Is everything okay?"

The question throws me off guard. I hesitate for a moment. Where do I begin? I let out a long breath and it all spills out: the attacks early in the year; the Spark; my suspicions about Elspeth Sinclair; and Cameron's half-brother.

Sophia's blue eyes have grown wide beneath her thick black bangs. "Wow! You've got a lot going on! This is a lot to absorb." She shakes her head. "What a sudden turn of crazy drama. You poor thing, having to deal with all of this crap, and when you're pregnant, too!" A bright smile spreads across her face and she squeals, "But you're going to have a baby! A little girl! Congratulations, I'm so happy for you!" She jumps up from her chair and envelops me in a crushing hug.

"Take it easy, you're smushing her!" I laugh. Sophia's joy is contagious. The Spark pulses brightly within my belly, and I sense that her spirit is lighter, as well. I have been so worried about protecting her that I have forgotten that what I *should* be feeling is happiness. I am going to be a mother. Cameron is going to be a father. And I know that he will be elated when I tell him the news.

I have been living in such a dark place in my mind, I had forgotten that congratulations would be forthcoming.

"I'm sorry," I say. "This is the first time I have allowed myself to be thrilled about this. With everything that has been going on, I've just been feeling anxious and unsettled."

STUFFED ANIMALS

"Well, I can see why. I would feel that way, myself." She squeezes my shoulder sympathetically, then pours herself a fresh coffee and sits beside me at the table. "I get how it is hard to trust Cameron right now, given that he may have injuries that he is oblivious of that are contributing to the situation."

I release a heavy sigh. "I love Cameron. But it isn't just that he may still have leakage due to his head wound and getting zapped. He has this innocence, a naiveté, which allows him to trust people outright when he doesn't know their intentions. I mean, it's good, in a way. But there are a lot of characters out there who will take advantage of that."

"I don't blame you for being suspicious. I have to agree with you. Neither of you knows who this Quinlan person really is," Sophia says.

"At least I feel that my paranoia is somewhat justified."

"It's definitely justified, Bishop. Since you are aware that he is a transmitter," she says, seeming to choose her words carefully, "Have you considered that he, himself, may be a cause for your overly angry reaction to Cam this morning?"

I stop and think about what she said for a second. Then I groan and slap my forehead with the palm of my hand. "Of course! I should have figured that out! I bet you're right. That would explain my overreaction. I could be receiving from him without knowing it."

She raises her eyebrows. "Well... and that you're pregnant. Probably everything will seem different than normal."

"I know he has this power. Half-brothers, be damned. They could be twins."

"Really," she says. "Is Quinlan single?" I give her a look, and she laughs. "Sorry, just kidding. Really, It doesn't matter whether he is, anyway, because *look!*" She waves her left in front of my hand. I see the shimmer of the gold and diamond engagement ring.

I gasp, my mouth gaping open like a largemouth bass. "Oh, Sophia! He proposed? Congratulations!" It is my turn to lean over and engulf her in an iron hug. "Have you set a date?"

"October sixth, next year."

"Well I have to say, it's about time! I'm so happy for you! Where?"

"The Lakeside Inn."

"Aww, that's going to be perfect, with the fall foliage."

"Will you help me plan?"

Her request catches me off guard. "Well, sure. But I thought you had a whole posse of girlfriends, and your mom."

She flaps her hand dismissively. "Mom and I aren't getting along so well."

"Oh? I thought you had reconciled."

"It was short-lived."

"Okay. And your buddies?"

"I really don't have as many as you think. One of them is out of the country. Another is kind of tied up with working full-time and raising two kids, and I feel like I would be overburdening her if I asked her to try to squeak out extra time for this."

"Okay. And the others?"

"The 'others' is *you*."

"Well, okay, then! I will be happy to help!"

Sophia beams. "We have so much prep to do! Our families are expanding! We need a baby shower and a bridal shower."

I smile. The Spark pulses in golden happiness.

I begin to understand how my moods affect her.

We grow quiet. I re-read my new orders. I am getting ready to go to the basement when Sophia stops me.

"Do you have a male to confide in? Some muscle? I mean, maybe your suspicions are baseless, but chances are that you're right. Do you have someone you can fall back on for protection if anything happens?"

I think for a minute. "Thank you for asking that. I hadn't considered it, but now I will. It's a good idea. There is an entire community out there that I can trust. I just don't want to be blabbing all over the place and then have Cameron find out that I couldn't trust in him, my own husband."

"But for good reason. Maybe you should at least come clean with him about your fears about Quinlan. And you are getting fuller in the face. You're going to have to go shopping, soon, and Cameron is going to notice. You should find a way to tell him before he figures it out for himself."

I squeeze my eyes shut. "I know I need to tell him. I *want* to tell him, but I don't know when would be the best time. We just had an argument this morning, and I fear stressing the baby."

"Please tell someone. Maybe Georgie, or Billy Tanner."

"Uh-uh, not Billy. I don't want him involved in anything. He has a family that needs him, not to mention his own brand-new baby. If the situation gets dangerous, I don't want to see anything happen to him."

"That's true. But at least tell Georgie – or someone else who can offer you protection."

"I will. That's a really good idea. But first, help me load the Jeep."

We descend the basement stairs and I check my new jobs that occupy the freezers. There are two red foxes, a rabbit, a pretty pet corgi, a beaver, two squirrels, and a male and female wood duck. All have been shrink-wrapped and frozen "I'll take four today. I'll get the other five when the first four are finished. Which ones are the oldest?"

Sophia helps me load the coolers that I keep in the back of the Jeep.

"I'm glad I got away from home for a while. I feel so much better. Thank you for the perspective."

Sophia laughs. "You don't come to your shop enough. I am always happy to see you."

"Same, here."

Glad to have gotten my troubles off of my chest, I hop in the Jeep and stop at Billy Tanner's just long enough to unload the coolers, then drive back to the 27. I bypass the A-frame and notice that Cameron's Note is gone.

Nine

*A*s I unlock the door to my workshop, Pepper trots out of the woods to greet me. I lean down and pet his head and scratch between his ears as he tilts his smiling, pointed face up to look at me. We enter the workshop together.

The gloom within reflects the clouds without, and it feels a bit chilly, so I start a small fire. Despite my antipathy toward the over-bright fluorescent lights, I had them installed to increase my working hours, as the oil lamps don't provide enough light for me to work far into the night. I only use the fluorescent lights when necessary, relying on the oil lamps and daylight the majority of the time. Today, I leave them off.

I grew up with my father's ways. Even with electricity to be had, he preferred more organic ways of doing things, and I have accepted my own old-fashioned tendencies. I have never felt in sync with the modern world and its encroaching technologies. Privacy is more and more lacking. And while I have nothing to hide, save my special abilities, I do have something to defend. Myself. Cameron. And now, the Spark. Smart phones, smart cars, smart appliances. Everywhere in modern society, cameras line the streets. There seems no true freedom any longer. Except in Wilson Lake, and on the Wilson 27.

I intend to keep it that way.

STUFFED ANIMALS

Upon my work table, I lay the furs that I picked up at Billy's after my stop at Stuffed Animals.

I've been working on three small mammals for which I already have the forms. All that needs to be done is the skins fitted on the forms and shape adjustments. Then I need to take care of the claws and eyes.

I work until well past dusk, driving the necessity to switch on the bright overhead lights. By the time the mounts are complete, I feel like my stomach is eating itself. I rummage through the fridge, gratified that Cam gave me extras to bring to the workshop fridge within the past couple of days. I put together a turkey sandwich with a little potato salad and pickle on the side.

I think about Cameron, wonder if he is okay. I admit to myself that I've been using my suspicion to cover up the fact that I simply don't like his half-brother. It doesn't matter whether he has something shady going on, a hidden agenda or ulterior motive, though I believe these things are true; I don't care. I don't like him. I don't trust him, and I am sure that he is here for no good reason.

Normally when I get strong negative emotions about someone, my senses are right on the money. I've gotten in trouble with people in the past more than once when I went against these intuitions.

I wonder how much Quinn had to do with the early spring attacks. I am convinced that he is involved, but I don't know exactly how. I feel that his sudden appearance is no coincidence and somehow has its place in the bigger picture.

If I could only *see* it.

I consider calling Cameron, but I still want to keep some space between us for a while, so I decide against it. I don't want any further confrontation or conflict, right now.

It wouldn't be the first time that we argued and spent the night apart. It wouldn't be the first night we've spent apart, even if we weren't arguing.

Occasionally, when I feel the need to be alone or if I have a lot of work to do, I stay the night at the workshop. I have an old sofa in the back room that I crash on if I'm working late into the night and too tired to make my way back to the A-frame.

Cameron always knows where I am, either way.

The phone rings while I am brushing my teeth. I think about ignoring it. I know it is my husband; no one else has need of the number. I don't want to speak to him. I have cooled down a bit, but I am drained from the strength of my earlier emotions. And I'm afraid that I might say something I can't come back from.

To keep a connection with him, despite how tenuous, I pick up the phone.

"Vix?"

"Hello, Cameron,"

"It's getting late. I take it you aren't coming back to the house tonight."

"No. I don't like the way that I'm feeling about us right now." Remembering my earlier conversation with Sophia, I keep in mind that that the situation has most likely been facilitated by Quinn. Not only has he influenced Cam, but it's entirely possible that he has also swayed my emotions.

"Bishop, I'm really sorry. I didn't know that what I said would make you feel the way that you do. I didn't mean what I said to sound the way it did."

He's apologizing, but only for the way I reacted to him. Not for what he said. "Okay, then, whatever you're talking about. But I don't want to be patronized. I'm not an idiot."

"I know you're not. And I know I have an arrogant streak. It's a part of me that just comes out, sometimes. But my questions were honest and didn't come from pride or arrogance."

"Okay, Cam. But I don't want to talk right now. As you said, it's late. And also – maybe you should give further consideration where those questions really did come from."

"When can we talk? Will I see you in the morning?"

"I can't answer either of those questions right now. I've got some things to figure out, and I'm too wiped out for a discussion."

A sigh from the other end of the line. "Okay, Bishop. Hopefully it will be soon."

I wait through the silence.

"Well, okay. Just make sure you lock up. Sleep well. I love you."

"I will. I love you back."

STUFFED ANIMALS

I hang up the phone, knowing that Cameron is feeling unsettled and fearful. But I can't ease his fear. I can't even comfort myself, right now.

The underlying seed that has grown in my mind is the idea that I may have been groomed and manipulated toward a lifetime with Cameron. I have always thought that I loved him, ever since we were children. I had thought it the natural course of events that we grew up and got married. I've never thought that the impermanence of my other relationships might have been deliberate.

Now I feel differently. I question our entire marriage. Is my love for Cameron induced and artificially grown? Or is it real? And if it was deliberately nurtured to sway me into marriage with him, does it matter? If it is true, can I return to our relationship with that knowledge and still flourish with him?

Do any of these questions matter, at this point?

I have never scrutinized my feelings toward my husband. They are emotions, after all, and I have never felt that my emotions qualified to be analyzed. I can't make decisions based on how I feel. I have always believed this. I feel like an idiot, now, thinking too much about how I "feel" and not objectively viewing the situation at hand with reason and logic.

I shake my head. I need to put this away for the night.

I lock the door and check the windows. I leave the dying fire to burn out and retire to the sofa and blanket in the back room.

I am deep in slumber when a pounding noise drags me up from the dark and relieving depths. The transition is so sudden that I lay for a few seconds, sweating and trembling, unsure that I had heard anything, at all. My stomach turns, just a little.

Pepper sits up at the foot of the sofa. He is mute, but the tension is evident in his alert body.

Then it comes again, a knock at the door.

I get up and pull on my robe, wondering why Cameron is knocking on the door instead of using his key. Thinking he might have just forgotten it, I turn the lock and pull the door open. "Cameron, I told you-"

But it isn't Cameron standing on the other side of the door.

It is his half-brother, Quinlan Winter.

I immediately pull up my protective shield. "What are you doing here?" I pull my robe closed and tie it tightly.

"May I come in?"

"Uh, no, you may not," I tell him. "Pepper."

The fox comes to stand before my bare feet, between me and Quinn.

"Why are you here? And how did you know that I was here?"

"Cameron gave me a tour when I was with him earlier today. He told me you were working here."

I cross my arms in front of me and add a thick layer to my protective shield, keeping my mind blank. "And?"

He shrugs. "I wanted to talk to you."

"And you had to come out here at who knows what hour? Couldn't you approach me in the daytime, like a normal person?"

I feel his energy reaching out, probing against my shield. Undoubtedly he identifies it for what it is. If Cameron can detect it, Quinn can, even more easily.

The turning in my stomach grows more pronounced. I am hungry – too hungry, and my stomach is rebelling. I begin to sweat from the nausea.

"Because I really need a moment of your undivided attention," he says and looks directly at my belly.

"Quinn, right now is *so* not the best time."

"I'm sorry, Bishop. I really don't mean to intrude-"

A sudden bout of lightheadedness causes me to sway. I feel sick.

Quinn steps forward across my threshold and reaches out a hand, presumably to help steady me. Pepper lunges, fixing his teeth on Quinn's hand in a warning bite. Quinn looks down at the fox, who remains motionless, his teeth fixed in place. "Is this really necessary? I mean, it doesn't hurt, but I just want to make sure you're okay. Do you need my help? Do you need to sit?"

I push at him weakly. "You need to leave. He's doing what he needs to."

I feel so exhausted. Then, remembering who is at my door, I reach as far down inside me as I can and pull up more resistance.

The exhaustion lessens, as does the nausea.

"Can I get you something? Water?" Quinn persists.

"No. I keep telling you. Quinn, you need to leave. Right now."

The only illumination comes from the glowing coals in the fire.

I am having difficulty reconciling the way Quinlan's pale face looks in the shadows, the way his dark hair curls down onto his forehead. He looks so much like my husband.

Whom I suddenly, desperately miss.

Quinn is making no move to leave. I put up both hands in a defensive gesture and dig down again for strength and resistance. I can feel his relentless energy pushing at me.

"I have something to say," he says.

"Why don't you do it from the other side of the door?" This time I step forward and summon extra strength. The Spark glows brightly for a split second, and suddenly, without my having touched him at all, Quinn is once again on the far side of my threshold. I don't see him move – he just *has*.

Pepper has let go of Quinn's hand and sits before me, once again.

Quinlan looks surprised. He clears his throat, and his face becomes expressionless. "How much has Cameron told you about me?"

"Not very much. Just what he knows. You were supposed to have died as an infant, but that your mother actually took you away and raised you."

"Anything else?"

"No."

"He didn't mention that I am our father's firstborn son?"

"No. He has always thought of himself as your big brother."

"That is an error. I am the older sibling."

I look at him, puzzled. "Okay. So what does that have to do with me? Why this behavior?"

His eyes are dark pools against his pale face. "It means that I am the firstborn son. That my mother took me and ran because I was born out of wedlock. Cameron was our father's legitimate son." He leans forward, staring at me intensely, but I have made my defenses solid, and he isn't gaining purchase to sway my emotions. "It means that everything that Cameron has experienced should have been my experience. As the elder male child. His education, his training, his upbringing and all that he has, now." He looks at me in the silence.

Does he mean the Wilson 27? The A-frame? But these come from my family. Not theirs. This is ridiculous.

"I don't mean to be rude to my husband's long lost brother, but are you kidding me right now?"

"I apologize, Bishop. I know that you aren't well, I know that it is inexcusable for me to just show up like this, but I just wanted to see you. To tell you. With our fathers long gone, there is no one to go to for a remedy. I should have been in Cameron's place."

Finally, I realize what Quinlan is saying, and also that he is living in a dream world. "But that isn't what happened. What's done is done. Cameron and I are married in a union recognized by the law of God and man. Not only this, but we are very much in love. Your claim is ridiculous. I think I know what you're getting at, and I am not property to be handed to whichever brother came first. This is the twenty-first century and things don't work that way anymore."

He smiles, and I am struck again by his resemblance to Cameron. "You're forgetting that you are the subject of an arranged marriage," he says. "But as far as your union with my half-brother goes, I was somehow hoping that you would reconsider that position. Wait – before you say anything else, I'll just leave. Okay? I knew when I came here it would be a long shot. But what the hell." He shrugs and begins rubbing the back of the hand that Pepper bit. "It was worth a try. It's a pity you never got to know me when we were young. It would have been nice if you had been allowed a choice. You could have chosen me."

I say nothing.

The silence grows long. Eventually Quinlan steps forward once more and leans over me. Pepper stands, but makes no move. "I would have liked to have had you as my wife, green-eyed lady," he whispers.

A wave of heat rolls through me. I can smell him, the soap from his shower, his aftershave, his deodorant. Not Drakkar. A different, heady scent. I feel my heartbeat speed up, and the

Spark's glow darkens with a resentful shade. I take a deep breath to calm myself.

He leans forward, touches my hand and brushes his lips against my forehead. I immediately feel a tiny jolt, together with the edges of Pepper's teeth as he bites Quinn, once again.

The steady pressure that I have been feeling ever since I opened the door builds. Quinn's energy is strange and frightening. Where Cameron's persistent transmissions are light and steady, easily translated, Quinn's are dark, intense, and powerful.

Dangerous. He is transmitting at a frightening volume.

I need to get him out of my workshop, out of my space. For the second time, I shove him away. This time, my gesture is also backed by my anger, as well as whatever energy the Spark contributes; her glow intensifying righteously.

He stumbles backward, nearly falls.

"You came here to tell me that because you are older than Cameron, you are entitled to his life? And that includes *me?* I'm sorry, but I am not and never was part of Cameron's or your 'birthright'. My decision to marry Cameron was mine. And to come here to fight over me? Dude. I am not important enough for you to be obsessing over. You've got serious issues, and I suggest you go find help."

"You don't even know what you are!" He retorts.

"Oh, my God! Goodbye!" I slam the door in his face. The entire workshop trembles with the force. *Oops*, I think.

Quinn laughs on the other side of the door. "You will be seeing me again," he says.

"Not if I can help it."

There is a long moment of silence, and I wonder if he has left. I am disappointed when he begins talking again.

"By the way. Not to be nosey, but if you love Cameron so much, why aren't you with him right now? Why are you staying out here by yourself? And why haven't you told him about the baby?"

I answer him with silence.

"Until we meet again," he says.

I lock the door and drag myself back to the sofa. If he has anything else to say, I don't intend to hear it.

"What is with you, Pepper? You couldn't tear off a chunk of flesh? I know you tried, but your effort was a little half-hearted, don't you think? But thanks for the thought."

Pepper gazes at me, then curls up at the foot of the sofa.

I toss and turn, trying to forget the things that Quinlan said, trying to forget the intensity of his energy. I realize that my reaction is only to what he was pushing; I feel no more attracted to him than before. In fact, I feel more repulsed. I've done nothing wrong. I haven't cheated on my husband, nor have I desired to.

Besides this, I feel that I am totally not worth all of this fuss. It's just a lot of drama over nothing at all. Why doesn't Quinn go find some other woman to obsess over? He is obviously not right. He's deranged.

All of this is just bizarre.

I finally fall into a restless sleep.

I dream that I am wrapped tightly in Quinlan's arms as he kisses me passionately.

I startle awake.

Now I feel guilty, though I am aware that this dream is just a residual effect of Quinlan's influence.

Unless he can transmit to me while I am sleeping.

This thought is not at all comforting. As I reflect upon the two parallel conversations that I've had with both Cameron and Quinlan, a seed of suspicion plants itself in my mind and begins to grow.

Ten

*E*ventually I fall asleep, only to wake to daylight a couple of hours later, still tired, but unable to stay on the couch any longer.

I rekindle the fire, glance out the window. A gentle rain falls. Rivulets of water roll down the glass and drip from the tree branches on to the glistening carpet of orange and red leaves below.

Hot coffee mug in hand, I review the work that I accomplished yesterday. I compare the forms to the photos of the animals. The three are ready.

I put the fire out, lock up, and take the Jeep back to the A-frame. I still don't really want to talk to Cameron, but I want to find out for sure where he picked up the ideas that he had expressed to me.

His Note is in the driveway.

The kitchen is dark, so I push through the door into the living room. And there they are, both of them, sitting on each end of the sofa.

Two identical heads swivel, two identical faces look at me, one with brown eyes, the other, yellow topaz. A chill skitters down my spine. This scene is too surreal. I feel like I have been absorbed into a *Twilight Zone* episode.

"Hey, Vix," Cameron says. His tone is measured, and immediately I know that he and Quinlan have discussed me.

"Bishop," Quinn says with a slight nod.

"What's up, boys?" I say, trying to sound more nonchalant than I feel.

The Spark is agitated. She pulses like a heartbeat, deep inside my abdomen. She glows brightly, but not with happiness; more of an anxiety. This is a warning.

I must tread lightly, here.

I strengthen my shield and extend my mental antennae. I listen to the environment and hear the conversation in the room before I entered.

Whispers form in the air around me. Quinn's voice. *"It wasn't her fault. Not really. She might just have wondered what someone else would be like. And we look so much alike."*

I still and quiet my breathing as I listen to the memory of the past conversation that Cameron is leaking.

"Oh, we're just hangin'," Cameron says. He is holding an open beer bottle, as is Quinn. I resist the temptation to glance at the mantel clock. "Have you gotten some work done?"

"I've nearly completed three more mounts, and I have nine more that have come in." I lower myself into my favorite overstuffed chair.

"We've been having an interesting conversation," Cameron says.

"Oh, have you?"

"I don't believe it," Cameron's ghost-whisper responds. *"Bishop loves me. She has never so much looked at another man. She is fiercely loyal."*

"How can you be so sure? Just a taste…"

Just a taste…a taste…

The words fade and evaporate into the poisoned air.

Quinlan has been whispering in my husband's ear, playing devil's advocate, telling outright lies.

"Yes," Cameron says. "Quinn has explained to me the nature of your relationship."

"I'm sorry?"

"I came out to see you at the workshop last night. I missed you. I was going to ask you to come home. But before I reached the door, guess who was just leaving?"

"Oh, I can tell you who. Your half-brother, there, showed up uninvited in the wee hours of the morning and attempted to glamour me into leaving you."

"Oh, stop pretending, Bishop," Quinn pipes up.

Cameron clears his throat. "So Quinn explained to me what happened." His face crumples. "How could you, Bishop? How could you betray me like this?"

An adult male in tears is always difficult to look at, but seeing Cameron break down like this is downright unwatchable.

"What are you talking about? What the hell did he tell you?"

"I told him that you invited me to your workshop, and I accepted your invitation. And I told him what happened when I came to visit you. Where would you like it to go from here, Bishop?"

"How *dare* you manipulate my husband this way! Cameron, whatever he told you is a lie. He came to the shop *uninvited*, banged on the door, woke me out of a sound sleep. I thought it was you. If I had known it was him, I never would have answered. Obviously opening the door was a mistake."

Cameron looks at me. "I don't know if I can believe you."

I look at his expression. Tearful, but dull. Not quite all there.

Then I turn to Quinn. He is smirking, staring at Cameron, pushing energy, transmitting.

Then I know that I can't win this battle. Cameron is completely submerged beneath his half-brother's influence. I have no talents or gifts that can combat this. I can only protect myself, not anyone else.

I try, anyway. "Cameron, how can you listen to him? You know me better than this. We've been best friends since we were toddlers! Wake up!"

"I thought I knew you. I thought I could trust you. The one person who would never betray me. But Quinn wouldn't lie. He's my family."

"*I* am your family! You've known this man for less than two weeks. How do you know anything he has said to you is true? You know nothing about him! You don't know who he is! We have spent a lifetime together! He is pushing you, Cameron. *Protect yourself*, damn it!"

He looks away from me and takes a swig from his beer. "I think we should go, Quinn."

Quinlan smiles at me triumphantly. "Whatever you feel like doing."

"Wait a minute, Cameron! How much have you had to drink?"

"Not enough," he says, rising.

"Stay, Cameron. You're angry at me for something I didn't do, and I don't want you to drive! Stay, please!"

He pushes past me. Quinlan follows. As he passes me, he whispers, "I'll see you later."

"I don't think so," I retort. I push in front of him, blocking his way. "If he gets hurt because of you, I will dismember you, limb by limb, digit by digit."

"Oh, promises, promises."

Cameron is already in the Note with the engine running. As he backs out of the drive, Quinlan waves to me and smiles from the passenger seat.

I am fuming, and the Spark is reacting to my emotional state. As I work to calm my hurt and anger, I reflect that I have needed to meditate an awful lot lately. The current situation aside, this may be my cue to step back, look at the big picture and do some soul searching.

I can't help but feel Quinlan's manipulations are related to the spring attacks on Cameron and our property; that this is all part of the same game. If so, he is acting according to a plan, maybe a Plan B or even C. It is now the beginning of August; the attacks happened in April. Whatever the plan is, it isn't a quick get-in, get-out scenario. Quinlan is in it for the long game.

I examine his motivations. I know that supposedly everyone has a twin. More than one look-alike, most likely. But from what I have seen, I am inclined to believe that he and Cameron both come from the same family lineage. Is it really as simple as Quinn told me? That he is the older sibling, and he believes that everything Cameron has belongs to him, as his birthright, and that he has set out to unseat Cameron and take everything from him?

I am not easily manipulated, but Cameron is a relatively pure soul. He can be easily swayed, as I have borne witness to, today.

STUFFED ANIMALS

Either that, or Quinn is simply that powerful.

I wonder whether Quinn knows that Cameron has virtually nothing to his name? His parents had gone bankrupt and relied on his marriage to me to make sure that he was taken care of. The Wilson 27 is my family's property, and my father made sure that we entered into an ironclad prenuptial agreement. The land will never be Cameron's unless I predecease him without an heir.

Of course, property ownership is all public record. Quinlan could easily have researched the chain of title to the Wilson 27. He may know that virtually everything we own belongs to me. And he knows he can't get to me, directly, so it makes sense that he would use Cameron in order to get to me.

Quinlan Winter has brainwashed my husband and has him completely under his control. Uncertainty over my family's future has my stomach tightened in knots.

There is also the question of whether Quinlan is acting independently. I think not. I believe that he has everything to do with Elspeth Sinclair. It may even be possible that she is his mother, or some other relative, and the two are in collusion. She may want the same thing that Quinn professes interest in: his birthright. And she may want what she feels she deserves is hers, as Cameron's father's lover.

But I don't think that's all. While we do have a decent nest egg, I am inclined to believe that they would want the Wilson 27 more because of its powerful geographical properties.

That could be enough to invite attack. Knowing this, I could re-classify them as power hunters. I would prefer they be gold diggers, instead. Because, if they are power hunters, they may not just be after the land. They might be after Cameron's and my gifts.

The thought chills me to the bone.

The Spark's existence reinforces the sense of horror that grows in my heart at the sheer magnitude of what Cameron and I might be facing.

Then indignation creeps in. Offended at the very idea that a couple of vagrant no-good sub-humans are attempting to destroy my family and our lives fuels my temper. I dampen the fire, secure the A-frame, and, following Sophia's suggestion, I take the Jeep to Georgie's.

Georgie Haskell and my dad were thick as thieves. They grew up together. There is no one else who has been more loyal to our family.

The diner is empty, the lunch rush having died down. Georgie serves me a meal on the house, as usual, and I explain the situation and my suspicions, starting with the attacks in April.

"What is your plan of action? You don't really know any of this for sure, right? The most you have is that this guy lied to Cameron to make him think you were having an affair in order to break you up." He wipes the counter down with a white cloth. "Although I think this is an effective example of 'divide and conquer'. I felt there was something funny going on when I first saw him."

"Was the first time you saw him that day with Cameron?"

"No. I saw him at the market with a little old lady. I thought he was Cameron for a minute, until I looked closer."

"Really? When was that?"

"Around spring time."

"As far as my plan of action – no. I don't know that any of my suspicions are true. But why cause a rift between me and Cameron? Obviously there is some kind of motivation, there."

"Maybe he has a crush on you, and wants you for himself. Covetousness."

"I doubt that anyone to go to so much trouble just for me. I think there is more than just mischief going on here."

Georgie shrugs. "I don't know, Mrs. MacArthur. You never know what drives a man to do the things he does. I think you are a prime motivator, but I gotta agree with you. It feels like there's more happening, though you are a part of it."

"I am not really sure what to do except to find Cameron and break the hold that Quinn has over him. Maybe in reverse order."

"Well, now that you've told me what you believe may be happening, maybe you should start checking in with me regularly. For your safety."

"That's a good idea. It will be a relief to know that someone is looking out for us."

"I'll put the word out, too, to some of my buddies. Most of them were friends of your dad's, and they will help us out. I'll tell them to watch for that Elspeth Sinclair, Cameron, and his half-brother."

"Okay, thank you, Georgie!"

"I'm happy to help. I don't want to see anything happen to you or your family."

I look down at the counter.

"I'm sorry," he says.

I shake my head. "Me, too."

"I think that I should come with you while you look for your husband. I don't like the way any of this feels. I don't trust it."

I feel some of the tension leave my shoulders, replaced by relief and gratitude. "Yes, would you, please?"

"I sure would. Let me make a couple of calls, first."

Soon, we are on our way. I leave the Jeep in the parking lot and ride with Georgie in his 1980s pickup truck.

We stop first at the Jermanic River Inn. The elderly gray-haired woman behind the front desk was one of my grandfather's good friends. "Hi, Mrs. Barron. Cameron's brother is staying here. Could you please point me in the direction of Quinlan Winter's room?

"Oh, yes, I've seen Mr. MacArthur visiting with Mr. Winter. Go on down, Mrs. MacArthur. Room 103."

"Thank you!"

We approach the room quietly, listening for signs of occupation. All seems quiet, including the Spark. The Spark recognizes her father ands always reaches out toward him, her light brightening, when he is near.

"Cameron isn't here," I say.

I reach out to knock on the wooden door. I feel the crackle of electricity when my knuckles connect.

"This entrance is warded."

"Will that keep us from checking inside?" Georgie asks.

"No, the wards are weak. More just for show. But that could mean either one of two things: he doesn't care enough about anything here to set a real trap; or it *is* a trap."

"What if just one of us goes in?"

I chew my lip in indecision. If Quinlan is as devious as I think he is, he would use concern over his warded suite as a psychological tool to increase my uncertainty. It is likely that he has nothing in his room, at all. My feeling is that there isn't. And if his wards were truly anything to worry about, I would have felt their power from several feet away.

I shrug, grasp the door knob, and whisper a few words. The door glows with red sigils and patterns. Token resistance that wouldn't even keep a lesser gifted out.

The knob turns easily and the door swings open, silent on its hinges. It might have even been left unlocked.

Georgie and I look inside. It is as I feared: utterly empty. The bed is neatly made. There is no luggage, nor any sign that the room has been used, at all.

We search anyway, through the bathroom, the kitchenette cupboards, the microwave, the dresser drawers. The housekeepers at the Jermanic River Inn have done their job. There is not a hair, not a fingernail clipping to be found.

Georgie is even more thorough than I. Long after I have given up the search, he is checking the insides of lampshades, the bases of lamps, the overlapping edges of the curtains, flipping the chairs over to examine the undersides, squatting down and craning his neck to see the underside of the desk. He checks the bottom of every drawer in the dresser, checks the bottom of the digital clock, pulls the drawer out of the bedside table and examines the entire thing. He separates each of the individually wrapped disposable cups on either side of the water bucket and checks between them.

I can't help but wonder what he is looking for.

When we have finished, there is not a square inch of the suite that has escaped our scrutiny.

"Wait. Look at this!" Georgie says, tipping one of the floor lamps at an angle.

I come closer and bend down. Taped beneath the base of the lamp is a key. I peel the tape back and both the key and the piece of tape fall into my hand. I feel a faint vibration when the metal touches my palm, but the sensation is there and gone so quickly that I dismiss it as imagination.

"What do you think that goes to?" Georgie asks.

I examine the key. How would I know? It looks like a standard metal house key. An idea pops into my mind, and I pull my key ring from my pocket and flip through my keys until I find one with a similar shape. I hold the two together.

They are identical.

"This is the key to our icehouse," I say.

"Why would Cameron's brother have a key to your icehouse?"

"You know about the icehouse, Georgie. You know it is the convergence point of most of the ley lines in New York State." I shake my head. "I have a really bad feeling about this. The fact that Quinlan has this key can't be good news. The icehouse stands upon a place of great power. Who knows what he will be able to do? Not only that, but if he plans on using the icehouse, why leave the key here?"

"Because he has Cameron," Georgie says simply.

My heart sinks. "Everything about this smells wrong. I was just at the icehouse. It was empty. But now I feel like I have to go there again."

"How much can Cameron's brother do if I am with you?"

I stop and look at Georgie. The hairs on my neck stand on end. The Spark flashes a tiny warning light.

I feel suddenly and unreasonably suspicious of Georgie.

"I mean, if all three of us went missing – Cameron, me, and you – it would be too obvious," he says quickly, as though he senses my distrust. "It would send up red flags. We are all prominent members of the community. And you and Cameron both – you are a couple, and the center of it."

I shake my head. I don't want to talk with Georgie any longer. I just keep seeing him searching through the room, through every miniscule detail. Like the undersides of drawers and bottoms of lamp bases. As though he knew there was something hidden somewhere.

Paranoia and suspicion are expanding above my head like a giant mushroom cloud. Something is not right, but I don't want to give myself away. If Georgie is in Quinlan's pocket, the gravity of the situation has increased a hundredfold.

The tips of the fingers on my left hand have begun to tingle against the metal of the found key. The Spark pulses a louder warning beat.

Something nags at me. Something that I should be remembering.

The numbness spreads slowly through my fingers, into my hand. I look at the found key in my left hand and my key ring in my right.

Then it clicks.

I look up at Georgie and I smile. "Would you hold this, please?" I hold out the found key to him. "I already have my own, but I think this might come in handy. I'd like you to keep it for me in case we need another."

He takes the key and pockets it.

"Let's go." I don't bother trying to repair Quinn's wards on the way out. I know he doesn't care whether anyone has entered the suite – that, in fact, he wanted me to enter.

I am desperately hoping that I didn't hang on to the found key for too long, as it is an iron key, most likely imbued with some kind of spell, and it touched my bare skin.

I realized this when the numbness started in my fingertips; and when I compared it to my own keys: each of my keys has a rubber cover over the bow, in case any of the metals contain iron.

As Georgie drives us back to the diner so that I can pick up the Jeep, I keep tabs on the numbness that travels slowly through my hand and into my wrist. My skin prickles with fear, and I try to keep my panic at bay. I don't know what manner of spell has been cast on the key, or how it will affect me.

Will it creep all the way up my arm, and when it reaches my heart, will my heart stop? Or will it travel up to my airways and suffocate me? Will it travel to my brain and wipe out my memory, or drive me insane?

I try to push these thoughts away as the Spark pulses redly in my belly. I work at focusing all of my energy into slowing, if not stopping, the possible poison that is slipping up my left arm. Had I held the key longer, I would be in much worse shape. Giving the key back to Georgie has helped to slow its effects.

Hopefully Georgie didn't notice anything amiss in my reactions when we were in Quinlan's suite. I am convinced that he is part of the overall machinations of whatever is happening, here; that he has been recruited into this to accompany me to the suite, to find the key and make sure it made its way into my hands. I don't know whether he knows anything about the spell.

At the diner, before I get in the Jeep, Georgie and I make a plan. He will allow me a head start to the 27 and the icehouse. Then he will follow me and, if there is trouble, will intervene.

In the Jeep, I speed back to the 27. Cameron's Versa Note is still not in evidence. I don't stop at the A-frame, but continue on to my workshop, where I grab my longbow and a quiver of arrows.

I am not entirely sure that Quinn and Cameron are at the icehouse. This idea came simply from the found key and gut feelings, based upon the same. If my assumptions are correct, I could play it two ways. I could "assume" that whatever Quinn's intentions are, he is bluffing. What if I don't show up at the icehouse, at all? What if I simply return to the A-frame and wait for Cameron to come home?

Given that this situation has culminated over the course of five months, I believe it is safe to assume that Quinn is *not* bluffing. It is safer to take him seriously. If I simply wait for Cameron to come home, I could be waiting forever. Quinn would force me to come looking for Cameron.

So I may as well just go look for Cameron at the icehouse and meet whatever might be waiting there.

The numbness has crept up as far as my left bicep, but seems to have slowed considerably. I am sure that I was meant to hold the key. If I had, I would have been debilitated by now.

My theory is that Quinn is using Cameron as bait to bring me in. The key was supposed to act as a neutralizer to reduce the chance that I will be able to use my abilities to fight him. I believe he thinks that if the key doesn't work, the icehouse's neutralizing properties will.

There is no cell phone signal on the 27, so I have no worries that Georgie is communicating with Quinn via phone. I'm not so sure about radio; I don't know how far a two-way radio signal would travel.

I drive the Jeep to a dense part of the woods located just out of earshot of the icehouse. I park it close to the stream which runs beneath the structure, but within a dense copse of trees, easily hidden from view. I set off on foot.

As I walk, I clear out my thoughts and shore up my mental and emotional defenses. I breathe deeply, emptying and focusing. I have a plan of my own that needs to remain invisible from prying minds.

I remove my socks and sneakers and step into the shallow edge of the stream, gasping at the water's cold shock.

The water will help to conceal my approach; not just by covering the sounds of my footsteps, but also by masking my energy field. With his advanced abilities, I am sure that Quinlan will be able to sense my presence; so the running water should render me virtually invisible, as well as muting the Spark.

As I pick my way through the stream, Pepper trots up and follows silently alongside the stream bank. He doesn't try to enter the water, though it is shallow and he is able to swim.

In the distance, I hear branches breaking and I see a large shadow moving between the trees. I know that this is Ursa Major, lumbering along. Her presence comforts me. I just hope that she remains at a distance, at least until I am closer to the icehouse. I don't want anyone to hear her and come outside to investigate.

The light-colored stone walls of the icehouse come into view. There are no windows in the building, so I won't be able to peek inside, and the stone construction effectively dulls sound, so it may not be easy to tell whether anyone is inside, and harder still to hear anything being discussed.

Cameron's Versa Note comes into view, parked beside the structure.

And if he is there, I can be reasonably sure that Quinn is there, as well.

While I am still a few yards away from the icehouse, I climb up out of the stream. I still myself, quieting further. I close my eyes and feel the ground beneath my feet: a combination of dried leaves, tiny twigs, and fresh dirt. I listen to the birds call in the trees and the deep sound of the clouds moving through the sky overhead. I focus on fading and blending into the surrounding environment. I can't do invisible, but I can do a passable camouflage. As I concentrate on the woods around me, I try to blank my mind. If there is nothing in my head, there is nothing for Quinn to pick up on – that is, if he hasn't already realized I am here. I draw energy up from the earth through my feet, and use it to form a tight shrink-wrap of a field around me.

Soon, I feel as ready as I can be. I don't know what awaits me up ahead – or whether anything is there, at all.

Still carrying my shoes in one hand, my bow in the other, my quiver over my shoulder, I move stealthily up to the rear exterior wall of the icehouse. The front door of the structure is the only entrance, and the door has a distinct sound. I will hear if it opens and anyone enters or leaves.

The Spark has begun to pulse a little larger, but quietly. Still, I tamp down her energy.

It won't hurt her to learn discretion at a young age.

Close to the wall, I extend my mental antennae. This is akin to listening really hard and hearing about 60% more than what many people normally hear. It's like putting a paper cup against the wall and leaning my ear against it, except that the cup is invisible and the sound is crystal clear.

I hear muffled voices. One is like Cameron's but not Cameron's, so I know it's Quinn.

The other voice is a woman's. Thin. Dry. Papery.

Try as I might, I can't make out any words. The natural acoustic properties of the stone effectively muffle the voices.

The Spark pulses a little quicker, becoming agitated. I catch sight of Pepper out of the corner of my eye. He is pacing back and forth beside me, but I am focused, so caught up in trying to catch any actual words from within the icehouse that I fail to hear the footsteps approaching.

I smell bacon, hamburgers. My quiver and bow are yanked away, and a cloth is pressed against my nose and mouth. Big arms wrap around me, holding my own arms to my sides. I immediately lose all muscle strength and coordination.

"Take it easy, Mrs. MacArthur," Georgie says. "Take it easy, and you won't get hurt.

Eleven

My feet are wet and freezing. My butt muscles hurt, and so do my shoulders and wrists. I am seated in a hard metal chair. My feet are immersed in cold running water. My legs and arms are immobilized.

I open my eyes and see that I am inside the icehouse. The wooden panel above the stream has been removed, and the chair to which I am tied sits in the stream. Correction: I am not tied. I am chained. My wrists and ankles are chained to the back and the legs of the chair. I'm sure the chains have some kind of iron component and are warded. My arms and legs feel heavy and numb.

In front of me is a man in a similar position: chained to another metal chair that sits in the stream, facing me. His frame is long and lanky, but dehydrated to the point of emaciation.

"Cameron!" My mouth is dry. My shout emerges as barely a whisper.

A woman sits on the floor beside the stream. Her palms are on my husband's cheeks, turning his head toward her, holding his face as she looks into his eyes. Her lips are close to his, nearly touching. Her hair is steel-grey, piled atop her head in loose curls. She turns briefly to look at me and smile. Her teeth are small and sharp; her eyes, dark, dark brown, almost black. A web of wrinkles covers her pasty white face. Two bright spots of rouge stand out in circles upon her cheeks. Her lips are painted dark red. She is dressed in an old midnight-blue tailored double-breasted coat with about a zillion buttons up the front, from beneath which spill what seem like yards and yards of flounced light blue skirts.

"You may as well say goodbye, dear," she says. Her papery, dry voice sends a chill down my spine.

She, herself, is ancient. She reminds me of mummified remains. This is Elspeth Sinclair.

She turns back to her task at hand, bringing her face back to Cameron's. Looking closely, I can see the air ripple: a transfer of energy passing from his mouth to hers.

I look on, my fear turning to horror as my husband's hair gradually turns grey, his cheeks sink inward beneath his cheekbones, and his skin turns papery and blue; while Elspeth's hair darkens to an almost purple auburn color. The lines and wrinkles in her face smooth out, and the thick paunch around her middle slims down a little.

Then I realize *what* she is, and my heart begins to beat double-time in panic. For a moment, I nearly lose my composure. Then I catch myself.

Elspeth Sinclair is fae. A fairy. A predator, and a formidable power hunter.

Lore paints fairies as dainty, tiny little good-natured creatures that flit about sunlit gardens like butterflies.

The truth is they are much like vampires, except they don't feed on blood to keep themselves youthful. They feed on humans' life-essences. It would be stereotypical to say that they are all ugly in both visage and spirit; most of them start out as stunning beauties. And some of them are kind.

But the ones like Elspeth Sinclair prey on the human race. Those like her seek people with gifts and special abilities who have reached the pinnacle of what it means to be what they are: artists, celebrities, singers, musicians; writers, professional cooks, scientists, mathematicians, doctors, athletes, and especially those of us with gifts that we keep hidden.

She has been draining Cameron dry.

"*Cameron!* You evil hag! Did you kill him? Cameron, *Cameron!*" I strain against the chains that hold me fast. I try to bump my chair through the water toward him.

She pulls her face away from him and lets his go; he sinks back into his seat, his head lolling limply. "Oh, he is still alive. But not for much longer!" she says almost gaily. "It is so nice to finally meet the legendary Bishop Bridgette Wilson MacArthur," she says. "I have heard so much about you. You, my dear, are a very special young lady." She glances at the two men who sit at a large wooden table: Quinlan Winter and Georgie Haskell. Georgie, who had been my father's best friend. To whom my father trusted my life.

"Georgie? What are you doing?"

Elspeth stands up and brushes off her jacket, inspecting both sleeves. "*George* is my great-grandnephew. Quinlan is my great-great-grandson."

My anger and my hatred become a lump in my throat. I want to snap this woman's neck with my bare hands.

"I will kill you. I will kill all of you for this!" My blood is boiling.

"Take it easy, green-eyed lady," Quinlan says.

"Don't call me that," I hiss. I hate him with everything that I have, every ounce of my being, for betraying Cameron and delivering him to the monster Elspeth Sinclair. "Cameron! Cameron! Show me that you're alive! Please, please show me!"

His eyelids twitch.

"I'm going to spare you, my dear. You are carrying a great gift." The old woman looks at my belly. "Your baby will be powerful beyond all belief."

"Don't even think about touching my baby!"

Cameron's eyelids open. His hands tremble. His taut lips open and a whisper comes out. "Baby…"

"Cameron, I wanted to tell you, but there was so much going on! I felt Quinn was influencing you; I didn't think it was safe!"

His eyes flicker to where Quinn sits beside Georgie at the table. Neither the table nor the chairs in which Cam and I sit belong in the icehouse. Elspeth and Quinn must have brought them.

STUFFED ANIMALS

I can't see the table top from my position, but the candles are evident, as is a chalice. I can guess that there must be a variety of other tools strewn across its surface: stones, oils, herbs, an athame, maybe some personal belongings of mine and Cameron's; other components for Elspeth's spells. No doubt they fear me and Cameron, or they would not have gone through such great lengths to render us incapable of protecting ourselves.

"What are you going to do? Just suck the energy out of us and bury us in the woods?" I ask.

The fairy bitch has the gall to look shocked. "Absolutely not, my dear! Do you think us barbarians?" The sight of her small, sharp teeth is unnerving. "I would never simply murder a woman who is with child. I am a mother, myself. Besides, the issue of yours and Cameron MacArthur's is sure to be gifted beyond even my own imagination." She claps her tiny, pudgy hands and says gleefully, "And I do so love babies!"

My heart sinks. The fae are some of the most heinous, bloodthirsty species that exist. And, as she said, they do love babies. Especially to steal human ones and raise them as their own. But I don't think that the Spark would have so benign a fate, should she fall into Elspeth Sinclair's hands.

"You're insane!"

"You can't live as long as I have and not be a little off, Mrs. MacArthur," she responds. "And my family *is* a little eccentric." That sharp smile again. "You should know, shouldn't you, dear? Don't you worry, though. Once I have finished draining your husband to an empty husk, we will repair to your workshop. It is so convenient that you have already outfitted it to be habitable, after a fashion. You will have all that you need and you will be comfortable and well cared for, in a familiar, cozy setting. You needn't be concerned about the baby. You will have the best care throughout your pregnancy. My son and I will stay in your humble little home – what do you call it? Your 'A-frame'? It is quaint, but doable."

"People will miss us. They'll know something is wrong."

"Oh, my dear. People rarely see your lovely face at all, to begin with. What is never seen can hardly be missed, now, can it? And as for your handsome husband – well, we have the perfect solution for that, don't we? No one will find you. And it won't matter. We will put your powers and your lands to a much better use than you, who hide like lowly cowards, trying to look like you 'fit in', when it's obvious that you don't even know that you belong to your own race."

She stands up and turns slowly in a circle, her arms open wide. "When we are finished, *my* family and *my* heirs and descendants will own these magical lands, and with your family's powers, we will start to build an empire on earth. No more wandering from place to place, no more nomadic lifestyle, no more lurking in between. We will plant our roots here, and we will plunder and pillage the human race, enslave them and feed on them! My Queendom!"

She walks around the table, comes to the edge of the floor where the stream runs through, leans over and looks down at Cameron's face.

"We are nearly done with him. His candle is nearly burned out." She lowers herself to sit beside him, as she had before.

I stare at my husband. I push my mind for an idea, something, anything, to get us out of this.

Magic is out of the question. Trussed up as I am, I am useless, and I have no transmission powers to persuade any one of these people to do my will. I can't send any subliminal suggestion out to any of our circle to have them come by and look for us; and even if I could, I don't know that we are within communication range of anyone. And if Georgie is a traitor, how many others are not true friends?

With this, my thoughts turn. Probably less of them than I might think. Elspeth has only Georgie and Quinlan to stand with her, here. If there were others, wouldn't they be present to help her?

I think of Pepper, trotting along beside me outside on the stream bank. I could yell to him. But then I remember Ursa Major, crashing through the woods, breaking branches. I can't send her a subliminal message.

But maybe she is within shouting range. If I yell to her, and if she hears me, will she even come? Does she really retain affection and a protective nature toward creatures that are benign to her? To humans? I think she does.

There is only one way to find out. I have nothing to lose by trying.

"Ursa Major!" my voice hits the stone walls and seems to fall flat.

Elspeth pauses, my husband's face between her hands. "What foolishness is this? No one can hear you. You're wasting your breath."

I ignore her and take the deepest breath that I can. "Pepper! Ursa! Ursa Major!"

The fairy bitch looks annoyed. "I hardly think that calling out spice names and appealing to the Big Dipper is going to help you, young lady. Those aren't even proper spells. Now quiet yourself or I will gag you." She turns back to Cameron.

The Spark glows a dull, throbbing red that I can almost feel burning inside my abdomen. A sudden surge of rage bubbles up from my belly to my throat. A veil of red drops before my eyes, clouding my vision. My fear and despair fall away.

How dare this monstrous thing dismiss me as though I am nothing? The audacity of this lesser being, traipsing into the home that I and my forefathers have built with the intention of draining all of it dry, exploiting and wasting it, and destroying all of those people that have helped sustain this lush mountain community – pisses me off.

Apparently, the Spark is not thrilled about it, either.

I breathe out fully and then inhale with everything I have. I hold it until my lungs feel close to bursting, my face red with the effort. When I can't bear it any longer, I let go of my pain, hurt, and rage in one long, high-pitched scream.

The sound echoes through the icehouse walls. I feel the chair vibrate where my ankles are chained. The vibration moves up through the chair, through my body, and spreads throughout the entire structure.

With a deep rumbling, the very earth begins to shake, and the wooden table jerks and pitches. Items roll to the edge of the table and crash to the floor, ceramic shattering, metal tools clanking flatly. A hairline crack appears above the door sill. It runs up the wall and across the ceiling. Small pieces of stone begin falling from the wall and ceiling, littering the floor.

"What is going on here?" Elspeth shouts. "George, Quinlan, outside, now!"

As they head for the only door, I hear a scratching noise from the other side; then a louder noise. Branches breaking.

Elspeth stills, listening. She looks at Georgie and jerks her head toward the door. "Go see what is happening."

Obliging her, Georgie opens the door. He shouts, not expecting what greets him. He staggers backward, struggling with something. He falls to his knees, and I see that Pepper has sunk his teeth deep into Georgie's throat. Georgie tries to pull the fox away from him as bright red blood runs down his neck

Major's body fills the doorway, the bear standing on her hind legs. Her huge mouth is open in a silent roar. Her long claws are splayed wide in the air. She comes back down onto all fours and rushes the door. The icehouse shakes as she hits the door frame. Dirt, chunks, and flakes of stone and mortar shower down around the doorway.

Major backs away and prepares to charge again.

"Quinlan! Stop that thing!" Elspeth is up and running toward the wooden table, presumably to try to find some kind of magic that will stop the bear.

Quinn stares at Major, concentrating. "I can't! There is no thought process! There is nothing there!"

"What?" Elspeth's face turns even whiter than her natural color.

And that is the last thing she ever says, because this time Major breaches the doorway, bringing pieces of it with her as she charges directly at Elspeth and Quinlan. She hits the fairy bitch first, taking her down amidst screams of terror and pain.

"Quinn, I can stop her if you let me out of these chains! If you don't, she'll kill you!" I shout at him.

Quinlan hurries over to me as Ursa Major savages his great-great grandmother. Blood, tissue, and bone shards splatter the icehouse walls as the bear clamps the fairy in her mouth and shakes her mercilessly.

If I were Quinn, at this point, I would run for Cameron's Note and get the hell out of there. Maybe he really thinks I will stop Major from killing him. But whatever is going through his mind, it doesn't matter: he unlocks my chains.

STUFFED ANIMALS

He then runs to release Cameron. After I help Quinn pull Cameron onto the icehouse floor, I limp to where my bow and quiver lie upon the floor. I snatch an arrow and nock it to my bow string.

I struggle to keep my footing as the earth shakes and shifts. The ceiling and walls are coming down. Chunks of stone, large and small, fall and roll, forming piles. Dust clouds rise into the air, catching in my throat and burning my eyes.

I aim. At a distance of barely ten feet, I can't miss, even with my vision obscured. The arrow flies true; I know this by his shouts of pain and surprise.

I run to Cameron and gather him in my arms. I can feel that he is nearly gone. I squeeze him tightly, pouring all of the energy that I can into him. Still affected by the chains and the running water, it runs fitfully, in dribs and drabs.

"Cameron, don't leave me!" Tears stream down my face. My body shakes with sobs. My nose is plugged with snot. "Don't leave us! I can't teach this baby how to use your gift! Who is going to teach her how to use your gift?"

Through the blur of my tears, I see Cameron's mouth working.

"I can't hear you!" I lean down beside him.

As his words escape his lips with a scarce breath, I get a faint image. He is tearing up a piece of paper. *"Shred it. Shred our agreement!"*

I suddenly understand.

Cameron has always been fearful of my gift. He made me promise, first when we were children, then again after we were married, not to ever resurrect him, no matter what happened. I made a solemn oath to him.

"But – I don't know if I can, Cameron! And you told me never, under any circumstances! I promised!"

The words sound inside my head as he strains to push them out of his. *"That was for when I was old. Or my body was destroyed. I want to live. I want to be a dad. Please, please, Bishop!"*

"I don't know if I can fix this damage!" And there is no time. Any minute now, the icehouse is going to completely collapse on top of us.

"Please! Use him!" His eyes flick over to where Quinlan lay bleeding.

I look at Quinlan. My stomach turns with loathing and bile surges into my throat. Cameron wants me to transfer his soul to Quinlan's body.

I have never done a soul transfer. I know how to do one, but in this case, I would almost rather put Cameron out of his misery, let Quinlan die, and raise the Spark on my own. The very idea of living with Quinlan's likeness repulses me. How could I ever reconcile myself to co-existing with the man who did this to Cameron? To us?

My mind feels as though it is bending. My rage is now focused upon my husband. This is all *his* fault. From the very beginning, *He* brought Quinlan and Elspeth to us. *He* has been the instrument of betrayal.

I want to kill him and leave him here. Wouldn't the Spark and I be better off without him than to live with blatant evidence of his errors in the form of Quinlan Winter?

The building groans around us. The walls list, and what remains of the ceiling tips at a slant, as though it is ready to simply slide away from the walls on top of us. I need to act, before we are all buried and it no longer matters.

I look back at my husband, at his elderly, drawn mouth, the cheekbones nearly protruding through the tissue-thin skin.

His eyes plead with me. They have darkened to a sick green-brown, and the light is receding from them fast. I feel the Spark, how distressed she is, her light pulsing in an almost bruised color.

My eyes fill with tears. I hate Quinlan Winter with every cell, every atom of my being. He is the most vile thing, other than Elspeth, that I have ever encountered.

How can I?

But Cameron's eyes are still pleading. *"Baby. My baby."* He touches my hand with dwindling strength. *"My family. I'm sorry, Vixen. So sorry."* A single tear runs from the corner of his eye down the papery cadaverous skin of his face.

The Spark glows pink. She is reaching for her father. She is pleading with me, as well, for me to show him mercy.

But what, exactly, constitutes mercy in this case?

I swallow.

I breathe.

What do I do? What do I do?

"I have to wait for him to die," I say.

The Note is closer to the icehouse than the Jeep. I search Cameron's pockets for the Note's keys. They aren't there. Cameron transmits a weak thought to me. *On the table.*

But they aren't there, either. I search the floor, scraping debris aside with my feet. I find the keys partially covered in rocks and dust. I scoop them up.

Cameron, his body depleted and shrunken, is easy to lift onto Major's back. Quinlan is harder, and Major sinks to her knees to provide a lower surface for me to load him onto.

"Major, run to the shop. Don't drop them!" She lumbers away through the doorway, Pepper running behind her.

I rush to the Note and peel away from the icehouse, spraying dirt as I crank the wheel to point me toward the taxidermy. The entire car shakes when I punch the gas pedal, and with a glance in the rearview mirror, I watch the icehouse collapse across the stream.

Epilogue

It is October, and Samhain draws near. This worries me. I had directed Major to drag Georgie Haskell well away from the icehouse and toward the border of the 27, closer to where he lived; and had her remove Elspeth Sinclair's remains out into the densely forested area within the interior of the Wilson 27, where the other woodland creatures picked her clean.

But I worry that their spirits are still close by, and they might cause trouble.

Cameron dismisses my fears. "They invited what they got," he says. "It was Pepper and Major that took care of them. Not us. Even if their spirits do wander around, they are bound to the 27. They won't be able to leave the property, and there is no one here but us."

When I express concern over their friends and family missing them, Cameron tells me that before I had arrived at the icehouse that fateful day, Elspeth and Quinlan had open discussions during which they disclosed a great deal.

No one knew they were at Wilson Lake. Elspeth possessed no identification. No social security number, no birth certificate, not even a purse or wallet. Because she was fae and not human, she belonged to the shadow lands alongside our physical reality. Due to her lifestyle - which consisted of kidnapping and sucking people dry so that she could remain youthful and then using her victims' assets to live well - she made an extra effort to fly under the radar. Unfortunately for her and fortunately for me and Cam, she succeeded.

Quinlan didn't exist, either. He lived by using his gifts to take advantage of others. No one ever knew his true identity. He hadn't led an established life anywhere. With Elspeth, he drained people of whatever resources they had and moved on, using false names and backgrounds.

"But I don't understand," I persist. "What about your student? Wasn't Elspeth her great-aunt?"

Cam shrugs. "Elspeth must have used brief glamour magic with my student. When I tried to get a sense of where my student's family is regarding Elspeth's missing person status, she had no idea who I was talking about. She has no great-aunt."

Neither of them would be missed.

And though Georgie had told me he had called some of his 'buddies' that day before we left the diner, he had lied. He had spoken to no one.

That still leaves me and Cameron as the last people to see him alive.

"If anyone finds their remains, it will be obvious that they were attacked by wild animals. As far as Georgie is concerned: you and I argued, I went with Quinn. Georgie drove you to look for me at the Inn. I wasn't there, Georgie drove you back to the diner. You got in Jeep and drove home, where you found me, we kissed and made up. You never saw Georgie after you left the diner. End of story."

"What will you say about Quinn if anyone asks?"

"He simply left. He went back to wherever he came from. It will be okay, Bishop," he says, when I still look worried. "You are the matriarch of Wilson Lake. Our people love you. We are a tight-knit community. Even if someone notices anything, nothing points toward you. The only body that you harmed with your own hands is standing right in front of you."

I let my breath out. "Okay."

* * *

"Dr. Simms says I'm fit as a fiddle," Cameron tells me when he returns from his yearly checkup a few weeks later.

"Did he notice anything different?"

"He sensed something. And he did say that I seem different. But in that vague way, like if someone gets a haircut or loses a few pounds. I think it must be the eyes. Hey, would it help you if I got colored contact lenses?"

I ignore the question. "Nothing about the scar on your back?"

"No. I don't think it is that noticeable. You did a good job."

I look down, staring at my book, which lay open on my lap. I have read the same paragraph three times. I still don't know what it says.

"Is something wrong?" he asks me.

"All of this is wrong. Don't you ever feel strange? Inhabiting your half-brother's body? Being with me?"

"What do you mean?"

I just blurt it out. "Do you ever worry that I am attracted to you? As Quinn? This is so messed up."

He sits beside me on the sofa. "Yes. I do think about it. But I know that everything that happened, happened because my faith failed you. I failed you. You tried to warn me." He takes my hand in his and entwines his fingers with mine. "And I know how you feel. I can tell. Remember?"

I do remember.

Because Quinlan had inherited his gifts genetically, they were in his DNA and remained in his physical body when his soul departed. He had refined his gifts, and was substantially more powerful than Cameron. When I transferred Cameron's soul into Quinlan's body, Cameron received those attributes. Now he is a transmitter as well as being a receiver, and he is much more attuned to me than he has ever been before. Now, if I want to keep my thoughts private, I have to make an extra-active practice of shielding.

Acclimating to Cameron's change is difficult for me. He can't understand. He doesn't think it is such a big deal because they looked so much alike.

But to me, the difference is as clear as night and day.

All the same, I am able to identify Cameron's mannerisms, his words and phrases, his personality, beaming through the face that is his, but not his. One day not long ago, as we sat down to breakfast on the back deck, the sun reflected in his eyes, and they were topaz. Just for a second.

After that, I say, "Remember when you suggested colored contact lenses? I do think that might help.

The most telling thing of all is that the Spark has always reached for Cameron, knowing he is her father. She never reached for Quinlan. For the brief time that he intruded into our lives, she remained aloof and guarded from him.

That is how I have become convinced that it is truly Cameron beneath the skin. The Spark reaches for him.

In the night, when we lay in the dark together, between the sheets in our comfortable, familiar bed beneath the skylight, I stretch my body along the length of his, from shoulder to ankle, my growing belly pressed against him so that he can feel the Spark rolling and kicking him.

Then he kisses me in the darkness, and I know it is Cameron, and it is okay. It is right. It is perfect.

"I love you, Vixen," he says.

"I love you back, Mr. President."

And I do. I love my husband.

THE END